The Ghosts of Gribblesea Pier

Gribblesea
Pier

ADMIT
ONE

887137

887137

887137

...tography
Gribblesea

ADM

The Ghosts of Gribblesea Pier

Deborah Abela

Farrar Straus Giroux

New York

Copyright © 2009 by Deborah Abela
All rights reserved
Originally published in Australia by Random House Australia
Distributed in Canada by D&M Publishers, Inc.
Printed in September 2011 in the United States of America
by RR Donnelley & Sons Company, Harrisonburg, Virginia
Designed by Roberta Pressel
First American edition, 2011
10 9 8 7 6 5 4 3 2 1

mackids.com

Library of Congress Cataloging-in-Publication Data
Abela, Deborah, 1966–
    The ghosts of Gribblesea Pier / Deborah Abela. — 1st American ed.
        p.   cm.
    Summary: Aurelie Bonhoffen, who has grown up in the circus, discovers a remarkable
family secret on her twelfth birthday that may help in dealing with a sinister man who wants
to take over their pier.
    ISBN: 978-0-374-36239-3
    [1. Circus—Fiction.   2. Eccentrics and eccentricities—Fiction.   3. Ghosts—Fiction.
4. Family life—England—Fiction.   5. Swindlers and swindling—Fiction.   6. Mayors—Fiction.
7. England—Fiction.]   I. Title.

PZ7.A15937Gho 2011
[Fic]—dc22   2010022517

For Claire and Lucy O'Mahoney

The Ghosts of Gribblesea Pier

The Ghost Train

The girl lay in her coffin with a faint smile on her powder-white face. She had been carefully laid out. Gentle hands smoothed down her white silk dress, combed her soft curls, and brushed on her makeup so that her cheeks looked like two faintly pink cherry blossoms.

"So very young," the taller of two undertakers mused.

"And beautiful," answered the other, a cruel scar running down his left cheek.

Framed by the flickering light of a candelabra behind them, they fussed around the girl, fixing a lone curl across her forehead, straightening out the black satin ribbon around her waist, and finding the exact place for a single white lily to lay across her chest.

They were never happy until everything was perfect.

The shorter man put his lofty black top hat on his perfectly combed hair. For today's ceremony he had chosen the one with the flowing gray band and white feather. He'd buffed it with a horsehair brush given to him by his grandfather, who had also been in the business. "We're ready," he announced with a flourish of his hand.

The other man's left eyebrow rose slightly. "You don't think you've overdone it a little with the hat?"

"I think it fitting." The shorter undertaker positioned his nose, just so, in the air. "It's dignified yet mournful, graceful yet not too showy." He scowled and mumbled, "Anyone with an ounce of fashion sense can see that."

They were twin brothers, born ninety seconds apart. The shorter, younger brother was never one for taking orders or advice from the older—never had been and wasn't about to start now.

"Fashion sense? You wouldn't know fashion if it walked down the catwalk and tripped you."

The rattling of a train in the distance broke through their argument.

"Right on time," they both whispered with more than a speck of delight.

The wheels screeched along the metal tracks. The carriages strained with the weight of passengers, crawling slowly through the pitch-black night. Eerie, creature-like shadows jumped out at every bend. The misty, damp air filled with the echo of hooting owls, the far-off screeching of vultures, and the hungry cries of nearby wolves.

Then they heard the first scream.

"Earlier than usual." The younger man pulled a watch from his vest pocket.

"Yes, but not one of our best."

"No, no, we must work on that."

For their work to be successful, everything must be timed perfectly. One slipup, one fall or stumble, could ruin everything.

Another terrified cry sounded, this time closer.

"Two screams." The older one adjusted his already perfectly adjusted jacket. "Death can be fearful."

Knife-sharp beams of light lit up the tunnel walls before them.

"Ready?"

"Ready."

The front carriage of the train loomed around the corner. The undertakers threw their hands up to their brightly illuminated faces.

"It's coming straight for us!" they cried.

The undertakers appeared to float into the air, as did the candelabra behind them. The lifeless girl between them suddenly sprang forward and screamed. An ear-stabbing, heart-piercing scream. A trickle of blood flowed down her forehead and from the murderous cut roughly sewn across her throat.

"Aaaah!" Whole carriages of screaming dread. One passenger fainted.

Within seconds it was over. The train swooped by. Flashes of sparks faded, and the screeching of passengers and metal wheels drew away into the distance.

The girl's voice erupted through the murky dark that remained. "That was our best yet!"

The taller undertaker snapped a handkerchief from his pocket and dabbed at her bloodied forehead and neck. "Your performance gets better each time, young Aurelie. What's not to scream at?"

"Thanks, Uncle Rindolf." Aurelie's teeth flashed from her pale face. "You're not so bad yourself."

The shorter one, Uncle Rolo, held his hat in front of his chest. "Nothing like causing a bit of a fright to get the heart going."

Rolo and Rindolf had sharp gray-black curls and impish faces deeply lined from entertaining audiences since they were boys. They'd stand with apples on their heads for the knife-throwing act, whinny and neigh as the head and rear end of a horse and, of course, terrify innocent passengers on the ghost train.

"We'll always be guaranteed a fright with that schnoz of yours." Rindolf threw a look at his brother as he helped Aurelie out of her coffin. "It's enough to scare a person into an early grave."

"You might want to look in the mirror before you

start talking about frightening features, skunkface," Rolo shot back.

Aurelie giggled.

"And don't you encourage him." Rolo waved a finger. "If he thinks he's funny, he'll never stop."

The echoing laughter of passengers seeped into the tunnel as they reached the end of the ride. It was the last train for the night.

"Even with my skunkface, I do enjoy a bit of fear-making." Rindolf nudged his brother.

Rolo's face spread into a reluctant smile. "And pants-scaring."

Rindolf shook with laughter. "We scared the pants right off someone once. Tell Aurelie how we did it."

Rolo blew out the candles and took a flashlight from his pocket. "I'd be delighted." He limped a few steps to the exit, held open the door for his niece, and bowed deeply.

Their faces became lit by strings of colored lightbulbs that crisscrossed their way throughout the pier.

"It was in front of the Bulgarian royal family in the capital, Sofia. We went there for a special performance at the king's invitation. We were warming up the crowd with some simple tumbling and balancing . . ."

"Rolo'd flip your mother into the air and she'd land on my shoulders. Nothing too fancy."

"But it did look spectacular," Rolo added, "because your mother would do it with two flaming torches."

All around them pier workers pulled down shutters on kiosks selling hot dogs, cotton candy, and soft-serve ice creams dipped in chocolate. Rindolf rushed over to the waffle stand, poked his head between the shutters, and minutes later withdrew three plates of steaming waffles topped with melting swirls of cream.

Aurelie and Rolo sat at a round table shaped like a teacup and saucer. The last of the patrons were making their way to the curled steel gates at the front of the pier. Groups of teenagers slung their arms over each other's shoulders, couples held hands, and young kids chased each other through clusters of deck chairs.

Rolo's eyes wandered over them. Searching.

Rindolf handed a waffle to Aurelie and shoved the other beneath his brother's absorbed look. "Are you going to tell this story or not?" He squeezed into the teacup with them.

"I was waiting for you." Rolo sank his fork into his waffle and stole one last look. "From up above, in the balconies where the rich people sat, a woman screamed."

"Ooooh, she was loud. I can still hear the ringing in my ears." Rindolf rubbed his ears exaggeratedly.

"She was screaming because this young boy—"

"Who couldn't afford a ticket—"

"Had sneaked into the theater and found himself a safe position behind the rather large skirts of this woman who had fallen asleep."

"Not all our audiences were cultured enough to appreciate art when they saw it." Rindolf sniffed.

Aurelie smiled through a mouthful of waffle and cream.

"But as the boy peered over the edge of the balcony," Rolo continued, "he laughed so much at what he was seeing—"

"We were funny," Rindolf added.

"That he fell back into the fine lady's lap. That's when she screamed. The chase was on. Everyone in the theater was determined to catch the intruder, but he swerved and dodged and, just as he was about to get away, a generously bellied gentleman caught him by the edge of his pants. The man held on, red cheeks puffed out, wheezing, until the boy undid his trousers and stepped out of them in front of blushing ladies, giggling girls, and loud shrieks."

"I normally hate being upstaged, but it was good sport." Rindolf nodded.

"What happened to the boy?" Aurelie asked.

Rolo smiled. "We found him hiding in a Dumpster behind the theater. He said his mother would have him whipped from one side of town to the other if he went home without his pants, so we sneaked back inside and found him a new pair in the costume trunk." He slipped a last morsel of waffle into his mouth and looked at the dwindling crowds. "There'll be a good ten minutes before the last of our guests leave and we have to lock the gate."

"To the roof?" Rindolf asked.

"Where else?" Rolo answered.

On certain evenings after they finished their work, when the wind wasn't too furious or cold, they would climb the stairs to Aurelie's room above the ghost train. Inside, the walls were hung with rich red theater curtains. Stained-glass lamps sat on handmade tables, while strings of tiny twinkling lights glowed across the room like fireflies. There was a large feather bed covered with cushions and soft toys, and nestled at the end was a trunk full of shawls, blankets, and costumes from years of the Bonhoffens' shows.

They reached in, grabbed a blanket, and climbed the ladder leading to a skylight. Outside, Aurelie huddled between her uncles.

"Can you feel that?" Rolo asked. "The wind's changing. Autumn's coming."

"And here I was thinking it was your flatulence." Rindolf scowled.

Rolo stiffened. "I don't remember asking for your flimsy, shriveled opinions."

Rindolf collapsed into a giggle.

"He's just teasing, Rolo." Aurelie kissed him on the cheek.

"I have a lot of valuable things to say." Rolo turned his back on them both. "I should have been in politics. I'd have made a great mayor."

"You'd have been the best." Aurelie nudged into him. "I'd have voted for you . . . if I'd been old enough."

"Me too," Uncle Rindolf declared firmly. "If I'd had the stuffing fall out of my head."

"That's it, I . . ." But before Rolo could storm off, Aurelie and Rindolf smothered him with hugs, tickles, and smooches. "All right, all right. Get off, you win."

"We always win," Aurelie said. "You love us and, no matter how much we annoy you, you always will. Admit it."

"Maybe." Rolo smiled and looked away, his eyes resting on the faint lights of a mansion on the cliffs at the edge of town.

"Why do you always stare at that house?" Aurelie asked.

Rolo buried his chin into his blanket. "I don't stare at any house."

"You do. That one on the cliff. You think we never notice but we do."

Rindolf nodded. "She's right."

"I look at lots of houses," Rolo said. "Sometimes I may wonder who lives in that particular house, but no more than the others."

"Sometimes?" Rindolf asked.

"Yes, sometimes. I'm an interested man. I like looking at things. And anyway, who wants to talk of old houses when we have Aurelie's birthday to celebrate?"

"Too right," Rindolf said. "Close your eyes, Miss Bonhoffen."

Aurelie did as she was told. After a few seconds of whispering and rustling, Rindolf said, "Open says-a-me."

He held out a cupcake with a single lit candle, which he shielded with his hands. "Make a wish."

Aurelie concentrated before blowing out the flame.

"And this is for you." Rolo took a small brown parcel from his pocket.

Aurelie untied the string and a gust of wind tore the paper away. Rolo snatched it from the air before it was swept out to sea.

In her hand lay a wooden replica of the pier with a small crank on the side. She turned it to hear the tinny notes of "Happy Birthday."

"It's perfect."

"Happy twelfth birthday, Aurelie Bonhoffen." Her uncles kissed her on both cheeks. Aurelie broke the cup-cake into three pieces and they shared it.

Rolo checked his watch. "We better be getting down. Gates'll need to be shut by now."

As the three made their way back to the skylight,

Rindolf tripped over his big boots and stumbled dangerously close to the edge. His arms windmilled, trying to steady his teetering body—but to no avail. He began to lean backwards.

"Uncle Rindolf!" Aurelie shouted.

Rolo's face creased in panic as his brother began to fall. An apologetic look filled his eyes, and he pushed Aurelie behind him. She spilled onto the roof, arms splayed to break her fall, and turned in time to witness Rolo pulling his brother to safety.

But there was something unusual about the rescue. It was as if Uncle Rolo's arms stretched further than their length should have allowed. And that Rindolf had fallen far below the edge of the roof, far beyond any chance of rescue, before he was hoisted upright.

"How did you . . . ?"

"Sorry about the shove, Aurelie." Rolo scrambled to help his niece up. "Just didn't want to lose you and my clumsy clod of a brother at the same time."

"Clumsy, yeah." Rindolf agreed. "Lucky you were there, brother. Not sure I was ready for a swim tonight."

"I thought I . . ." Aurelie tried again.

"We should go." Rindolf flicked his head toward his brother and rubbed his hands together. "It's colder out here than I thought. Anyone else cold?"

"It's cold. I agree," Rolo said. "Can't have Aurelie catching a cold on her birthday."

"But it's just that . . ."

"As much as I hate to admit it, Rolo's right," Rindolf said. "And that gate won't shut by itself."

The two uncles gently coaxed their niece down through the skylight and onto the ladder. They fidgeted and talked incessantly, smothering any chance of her speaking.

"That's it. In you go."

For all their attempts at covering what had happened, Rolo and Rindolf knew what Aurelie had seen, but it wasn't the seeing they were shivering about—it was dealing with their mother, Lilliana Bonhoffen.

"All we had to do was keep her out of the way until they were ready, and now we've mucked it up," Rolo whispered to Rindolf before he stepped down the ladder. "She won't be happy."

"She's been unhappy with us in the past, but this time she'll pickle us for sure."

The Party

Aurelie dragged at the curved and swirled ironwork of the pier's front gates. She lined them up, pushed the thick bolts into the ground, and threaded through the heavy iron chain. She had to use both hands to click the padlock shut, checking it with a good shake before turning back and running to her uncles. While they piled deck chairs into a small shed, Aurelie caught their whispered bickering.

"She's going to guess," Rindolf hissed, and handed Rolo another chair.

"She mightn't."

"She's a smart one; she'll work it out."

"Work out what?" Aurelie's eyes widened.

Rolo stopped mid-chair-lifting. "That . . . that—"

"She's the most beautiful niece an uncle could ever hope for," Rindolf finished.

Aurelie folded her arms across her chest. "Nice try, but I don't believe you."

Rolo clutched both hands to his heart. "Oh, the pain of accusations slung at my heart like arrows."

"Okay, Mr. Overacting, *who* is going to work out *what?*"

Rindolf loaded the last of the chairs into the shed. "It's late and you'd best be getting to bed."

Aurelie's shoulders sank. "Bed?"

"Yes, of course." Rindolf closed the door of the shed. "You have school tomorrow, and it's already nine o'clock."

"But I thought—"

"Wait," Rindolf interrupted. "It's our turn to check that the lights are switched off in the circus tent."

"You know, you're right, Rindo. Ha, I almost forgot."

Aurelie's smile lifted. This was more like it. She knew, of course, there were no lights to check. Her family had been secreting things away from her for weeks. They'd break from whispered huddles when she walked into a room and pretend to pack things into boxes as an early spring-cleaning effort. This was a dead giveaway. The Bonhoffens *never* did spring-cleaning. Each member of her family dreaded throwing things away: ticket stubs from movies, feathers, odd-shaped pebbles that resembled people.

"Every little thing you are given contains a part of the

person who gave it to you," Lilliana would say. "To throw it away would be like throwing a part of *them* away. To other people it may look like junk, but it's never just junk."

So it wasn't spring-cleaning.

Regally positioned, like a jeweled crown at the end of the pier, stood the big top. Its tall, pointed tips rose into the air at every angle and fluttered with flags and glowed with colored lights. This was where the performances on the pier were held—where clowns juggled, trapeze artists swung through the air, and fire-twirlers turned flaming batons that coiled as if they were alive.

"It's dark." Aurelie stood before the silent tent.

"Looks like the lights are off," Rindolf said.

"Let's go inside to be sure." Rolo pushed aside the canvas flap. "Come on, Aurelie, you go in first."

They followed her inside.

Rindolf shot his brother a sneaky smile before he threw a switch, which filled the circus tent with hundreds of tiny lights.

"Happy birthday!" The cry of a small crowd was punctuated by two cannons blasting confetti into the air. Balloons spilled from a net above, and strings of lanterns glowed beneath the canopy in bright reds, yellows, and blues.

"It's good we checked the lights after all." Rolo shrugged.

Aurelie threw herself at her uncles. "Thank you." She squeezed them tightly. "You're terrible liars."

"We'll take that as a compliment." Rindolf nodded.

Aurelie's father and mother stepped forward. "Happy birthday, Aurelie." Amarella Bonhoffen swept her daughter into her arms.

"You didn't really believe it was time for bed, did you?" Argus Bonhoffen winked at Rolo and Rindolf.

"I never know what to believe with these two," Aurelie answered.

Even though he'd worn his best suit, Argus always had an edge of scruffiness about him he couldn't shake—a gangliness with permanently wind-rumpled hair. He leaned down and kissed her on both cheeks. "But your party has only just begun."

Amarella had wisps of long, flowing hair that she would try to sweep into a bun behind her, but small restless curls would always sneak out around her face. She had a soft smile and eyes so alive that Argus would swear he'd be kept awake at night by the light tucked inside them. "Come this way," she whispered.

The small crowd peeled away into the shadows as Argus, Amarella, Rolo, and Rindolf led the birthday girl to the tiered seats of the big top. They stopped before a large object on a platform, hidden beneath a sheet. Beside it was her grandmother, Lilliana.

"Thought you were never going to get here." She smiled. "Let's see what's under this, eh?"

Aurelie grabbed the end of the sheet and pulled it away, revealing a wooden thronelike chair lined with soft, satiny cushions.

Aurelie gasped. "It's beautiful."

"Happy birthday." Argus held out his hand and helped her onto her queenly chair. Aurelie rubbed her hands along the silk-covered arms and wriggled into its soft, cushioned seat.

"Any room for me?" Lilliana asked.

"There's always room for you." Aurelie moved over. Her grandmother sat beside her while the rest of her family hurried to the orchestra pit. Amarella sent Aurelie a wink before lifting a fiddle to her chin. Rolo raised a trombone and Rindolf positioned an accordion against his chest, his foot resting on the peddle of a drum kit.

A spotlight trained on Argus in the center of the ring. "Let Aurelie Bonhoffen's birthday show begin!"

The orchestra launched into a high-paced tune. Argus only just got out of the way of a backfiring jalopy full of clowns. The contortionists followed, bending into impossible forms, tumbling and vaulting into human pyramids that seemed to defy gravity.

Aurelie and her grandmother applauded and

whooped before the band stopped playing and the circus tent snapped into darkness. A spotlight shone into the air, followed by another. The lights searched the roof until they settled on two raised platforms resting on the ends of towering poles. On these platforms stood To and Fro, the famous trapeze artists. The band struck up a grand *ta-da!* before breaking into a speedy melody.

Firmly clutching their trapezes, To and Fro swung into the air, gliding from an arm, a bent leg, sometimes from a single ankle.

Aurelie's clapping was interrupted by Rolo's drum-roll. To and Fro faced each other on opposite platforms. To held the trapeze before her. She took a short breath before launching herself into a deep arc. With each swing she gained speed and was soaring higher and higher. The band played faster until, with a single crash of a cymbal, To let go, flinging herself into a triple somer-sault. Aurelie gasped as To twirled and fell, sinking through the air until Fro, clinging to her trapeze with bended knees, swung out and plucked her from the air with strong, careful hands.

Aurelie jumped to her feet and cheered. Lilliana leaned over and whispered, "They've been working hard on getting that last bit right."

The lights faded to black. A small flame tumbled into view, followed by another, and another, until four fire-twirlers stood in the center of the ring.

In perfect unison, they swung their fiery batons in their hands, twirling them into blazing figure eights. They hurled them around either side of their bodies before throwing them into the air and catching them behind their backs.

A tall muscled man, whose arms were a canvas of tattoos, stepped forward.

"It's Enzo!" Aurelie shifted to the edge of her throne.

He threw her a smile and lifted his lit baton above him. He held it there momentarily, before dropping his head back and plunging it into his mouth. He closed his lips around the flames for what seemed too long, before pulling it out.

Aurelie and Lilliana rose to their feet, applauding and whistling and crying for more. Enzo bowed deeply. He laid the baton at his feet and walked over to Aurelie. He cupped his hands to his mouth and blew, waiting a few seconds before opening them out to reveal a flame dancing on his palms.

Enzo smiled, clasped his hands shut and reopened them quickly. The flame had gone, and in its place was a red gemstone.

"It is a star ruby." He slid the gem into Aurelie's hand. "When you hold her to the light, you can see a glowing star, like she has a fire inside her."

Aurelie held it up. "I can see it."

"Keep it close when you need to be strong." Enzo

held out a pair of long, fire-resistant gloves, decorated with bright orange flames. "Now it's time for you to join us."

"You think I'm ready?"

Enzo nodded.

Lilliana leaned over. "I guess that means you're on."

Aurelie slipped the ruby into her pocket and pulled the gloves up to her elbows. She took Enzo's hand, and he led her into the center of the ring. She tied her curls back while he lit four batons, handing two to Aurelie.

"Just like we practiced." Enzo nodded and they threw the batons to each other in a fiery two-person juggle. Flames swooped between them in glowing circles. Streaks of fire lit their faces as they threw them higher and higher, until Aurelie spun around in a rapid twist and held out her arms, catching both batons in quick succession.

Rolo and Rindolf led the cheers, whooping and hugging each other.

"I knew she could do it." Rolo wiped away a tear.

"She's a natural," Rindolf said, "just like I was."

Enzo doused the flames in a bucket of sand. He held Aurelie's hand high and they bowed to the applause.

"How was I?" Aurelie whispered.

"Not bad." Enzo's face stretched into a smile. "Now for the grand finale."

Rindolf played a drumroll from the pit. Each of the fire-twirlers lifted their batons. A flash of sparks ignited several fuses, sending snaking flames racing along a bent wire frame, curling and coiling.

Enzo slipped his hand into Aurelie's.

And there it was, blazing like hundreds of sparklers: *Happy Birthday Aurelie.* Argus wheeled out a small cart carrying a giant candle-covered cake and a wooden barrel.

"Black Forest cake and cloudberry juice. Your favorites," Argus said. "Lilliana made them."

Lilliana rushed over and kissed her on the cheek. "I used extra Belgian chocolate and the finest fresh berries."

"You better blow out the candles before they melt all over the cake." Rolo leaned in.

Aurelie blew a swirling pattern over the candles until every last one was out.

The party lasted until long past midnight, with singing, dancing, and enough cake for everyone to have three helpings each. Even when Aurelie's feet ached and her eyes strained under the tug of sleep, she refused to have it end. She sat in her new chair and closed her eyes for a moment. When she opened them again, she looked up to see the faces of Rindolf and Rolo, who were laying her gently into bed.

"Happy birthday, sweet Aurelie." As they tucked her in, Rolo took the star ruby from her hand and placed it on the bedside table.

"It seems not so long ago since she was born." Rindolf sighed.

"And now she's old enough to know the secret," Rolo said.

"Do you think she'll be okay?"

"She's our Aurelie. She'll be fine. I'm sure of it." Rindolf's smile was crooked and unsure.

The uncles took turns kissing Aurelie on the forehead. They stole one last look before tiptoeing outside.

The Secret

So she saw?" Lilliana Bonhoffen, it would be safe to say, looked a little peeved.

"Yes, but we're not sure what she saw, only that she saw something. Maybe it wasn't what we *thought* she saw, but something she saw that was quite altogether not what we thought she saw at all."

Rolo knew he wasn't making any sense and, even though he was a man in his forties, his mother had the ability to make him feel eight years old and in serious trouble.

There was a small knock at the door. Aurelie poked her head inside. "Argus and Amarella said you wanted me to have breakfast up here this morning."

"Yes. I thought it'd be a nice change."

Lilliana's room was above the ice-cream parlor—a building resembling a large cup of ice cream, complete with a glazed cherry on top. The parlor was located in the cup, with a swirling staircase on the side leading to Lilliana's room in the scoop of ice cream. Small heart-shaped windows in its rounded, bulging sides looked out over the sea, while letting in the smells of freshly made cones, wild vanilla, and rich, rich chocolate.

Aurelie gave her uncles an inquisitive look. Rolo opened his mouth, but Lilliana answered for them. "Your uncles were just leaving."

"Yes," Rindolf replied. "See you this afternoon at the train."

"Have a good day at school." Rolo blew her a kiss. Aurelie caught it and slipped it into her pocket.

"For later," Rolo whispered, and pulled the door closed behind him.

Lilliana walked over to a small kitchen area and opened the oven door. "Pour yourself some tea."

Aurelie dropped her school bag and drew her tired body to a table in the center of the room. She poured a sweet-smelling tea and sat on a small armchair. Her hair was wet from a bath that had done little to wake her up. She sipped her tea and let her eyes wander around Lilliana's room.

Embroidered cushions sat like curled-up cats on brightly colored lounges. Scarves hung from mirrors and stands. On a marble dressing table were bracelets, necklaces, and a twirling porcelain ballet dancer on a music box covered in gold leaf.

Every part of Lilliana's room told a story. Every trinket, dried flower, and postcard. There was a red silk sash from the king of Spain and a giant conch shell from the sultan of the Maldives. Shelves swept around the curved edges of the room and held leather-bound photo albums and armloads of books in different languages. There were racks flowing with dresses and handmade shoes threaded with sequins. Each object whispered stories of a young Lilliana riding plumed show horses, or performing on luxury ships. But Aurelie's favorites were the framed photos of her grandfather and grandmother in their circus days when Lilliana was one of the most famous performers in Europe.

"Did you enjoy your party last night?"

"It feels as if it only just finished." Aurelie yawned and slumped further into the chair.

Lilliana held out a plate of warm brioche lined with swirls of cinnamon. "Some of this might help."

She sat beside Aurelie in a chair not unlike Argus's present from last night. It was hand-carved so that turns of wood framed her like a crown, and it was lined with velvet. When Aurelie looked closer, she noticed it was worn and tattered in parts.

"We should get this repaired," she mumbled through a mouthful of brioche.

Lilliana stroked the frayed armrest. "Your grandfather made this for me as a wedding present. He sat me down, sank to both knees, and promised that all my life he would take care of me." She smiled. "He was an old softie."

"And you loved him for it." Aurelie popped the last of her brioche into her mouth.

"From the first moment I saw him." Lilliana flashed a cheeky grin. "He reminded me a lot of his brother, Lukash. Big, bold men who were very funny. The two of them were inseparable—had been since they were little kids. It was the saddest day of your grandfather's life when they nearly lost him."

"What happened?" Aurelie sipped her tea.

"They were swimming in the ocean not far from here. There was a strong current that day, and they were told not to swim out too far. Lukash was never one to be told what to do, so he waited until no one was looking and swam out farther. Pretty soon he was in trouble. The ocean gripped him like hands around his legs and pulled him out to sea. Your grandfather swam out to rescue him. Lukash struggled against the current, but he soon became tired. Your grandfather swam faster, but eventually Lukash gave up and disappeared under a wave."

"What did Grandad do?"

"His legs ached and his eyes stung from salty waves crashing over his head, but he wasn't about to give up. He forced himself forward, dived under and, through the churning sea, he saw Lukash. He swam farther down, grabbed him under the arms, and dragged him back to the surface.

"When they got to shore, he laid his brother on the sand. He tried resuscitation, but Lukash's skin had already turned a pale blue."

"He died?" Aurelie let her cup drift onto the table.

"You could tell by the looks of the passersby that they knew it was too late. Your grandfather held his brother's body and cried so hard you could hear it all along the beach. But then, Lukash opened his eyes."

"He did?"

"He gave a soft smile and said, 'Probably shouldn't have gone out that far.' Your grandfather laughed and hugged him so hard that Lukash had to tell him to take it easy."

"So he didn't die."

"Yes, he did." Lilliana took a deep breath. "Aurelie, I need to tell you something very important. About our family."

"Is something wrong?"

"No. Not wrong." She stroked Aurelie's hair. "For as far back as we can trace, the Bonhoffen family members have had a . . . gift."

"What kind of gift?"

Lilliana met her granddaughter's eyes carefully. "The ability to come back to life after they've died."

29

Aurelie paused. "Like ghosts?"

"That's one name given to them, but it isn't quite correct. Ghosts are spirits who were once human and appear to certain people, usually if they have a message for them. They're forever at the age they were when they died—but our gift is different."

"So what happened to Lukash?"

"It was later, when he was alone with your grandfather, that he explained it. He said when he was lying on the beach, he felt calm and quiet. He knew he'd died and was floating above his body, but he wasn't scared. What scared him was looking down and seeing how broken his brother was without him. So he decided to come back."

"He came back to life," Aurelie said, "just like he was before?"

"Not exactly. When someone comes back, they age as they normally would, and laugh and cry, and hurt when they stub their toe, just like you and me, but they have some of the marks of a ghost."

"Like what?" Aurelie's voice was small.

"They can become invisible, or levitate, or walk through walls."

"Walk through walls?"

"Only if they want to. Most of the time they open doors like everyone else."

Aurelie frowned. "So, the Bonhoffens can live for-ever?"

Lilliana laughed. "I'm not sure I've ever met a Bonhoffen who has wanted to do that. No, you only get one chance to come back. The next time you meet your end, it's final."

"Do all of us have it?"

"It seems everybody who was born a Bonhoffen, yes."

"Even me?" Aurelie's voice filled with a creeping fear.

Lilliana took Aurelie's hands in hers. "Even you. If you should ever wish to."

"Why does it happen to us?"

"Some say it can be traced back to the Middle Ages, to a distant ancestor in Scotland who was said to be a witch." Lilliana cocked an eyebrow. "An accusation people loved throwing at women back then. The woman and her son were driven out of town and became the first of our family to make their living as traveling performers. Others say the gift was given to them by a gypsy queen in Romania for saving her son from a burning barn. Maybe it's something we've always had."

Aurelie didn't move.

"The very special thing about this gift is that people never come back for small reasons, like a party they don't want to miss or a roast chicken they were about to eat. It's always for bigger reasons. Like love and friendship and knowing there would be someone too broken to go on without them." Lilliana smiled. "But mostly, it's for love."

"But then why didn't—"

"Because your grandfather was ready," Lilliana said. "He'd seen wars, met kings, survived sickness. His body was old and couldn't go on anymore." She paused. "Plus, I told the old codger he had to leave. He didn't want to at first, but I knew he'd always be with me, and I was right. There hasn't been one day when he's left my side."

"He's here?" Aurelie looked around the room.

"Yes. He's always nearby, making sure I don't trip on a crooked step or leave the stove on."

"Can you see him?" Aurelie whispered.

"Not now. I see him mostly at night when I'm falling asleep. He sits on the end of my bed."

"What does he do?"

Lilliana leaned in. "Juggles."

"Juggles?"

"He knows I love it. Each time he juggles something flashier—bottles, slippers, small octopuses. Not that the octopuses seem to like it, poor things."

Aurelie had been only three at her grandfather's funeral. She remembered bits. A black carriage with large, polished glass windows and white silken scarves sailing behind it like a regal ship. Horses, tall and black, breathing great smoky white puffs into the chilly air.

"He looks out for you too, you know." Lilliana smiled.

"He does?"

"Oh yes. Everyone has someone looking out for them—even the mean ones." She nudged Aurelie. "Your grandfather and I talk about you often."

"You talk to him?"

"The days wouldn't feel right if I didn't."

"How does it happen? The coming back?"

"When a Bonhoffen dies, there's a small sliver of time when you stand somewhere between life and death, when you can decide to come back to life. Lukash said it felt like hours, but when he came to he realized it was only seconds."

Aurelie's brows squeezed together. "So there are ghosts that are spirits and others that are half-ghost, half-human but who look and feel like us?"

"Pretty much."

"Is anyone I know like this?" she asked warily.

Lilliana nudged her nose into Aurelie's cheek. "That's not for me to say, but if you want to ask anything else, I'm all yours."

Aurelie shifted on her chair. A cold morning breeze sneaked beneath the door. Lilliana handed her another chunk of cinnamon twist. "But for now, you're off to school."

She slipped her hand into Aurelie's and walked her down the curved stairs of the ice-cream parlor, through the pier, and past a few early morning visitors.

At the front gates, Lilliana held her granddaughter's face in her hands. "The secret is hard at first, I don't pretend it isn't, but it is a gift not a curse. Something to be thought of as special, that sets us apart from the world."

She kissed Aurelie on both cheeks and watched as she hoisted her bag over her shoulder and made her way through the gates of Gribblesea Pier to school.

Aurelie Bonhoffen

Here she comes."

Three students crouched behind a bush inside the entrance of Gribblesea Academy. Charles was a smart boy with well-behaved golden locks who bored easily. The other, Sniggard, had never read a book, so forever felt a sense of having lost something important. The third was Rufus Bog, the mayor's son.

"Come on, Bog, don't chicken out now," Sniggard hissed. "If you wait any longer she'll be gone."

Bog's shoulders twitched. He stretched a slingshot in front of his eye. His hands shook as he held Aurelie in his sights.

"Now!" Sniggard commanded.

Rufus flinched and released the sling. The paint-filled balloon flew out of its rubber strap. The three boys held their breath.

The balloon ripped through the air—but not at its

intended target. It sailed past Aurelie, toward the up-turned nose and crisp, rigid step of Mrs. Sneed, the math teacher.

Charles gasped and Sniggard's face lit up with the delicious possibility of what might happen next. Bog swallowed what felt like a steel lump. Mrs. Sneed, her lips twisted in horror, screamed as the red paint splattered over her dress.

"Oh! What on earth . . . what in the name of . . . who ever has . . ." she spluttered, searching for the reason why her Monday morning had become littered with such *unexpectedness*. Mrs. Sneed, being a math teacher, always relied on the certainty of formulas, the logic of equations, and the uninterrupted quietness of her walks to school.

She didn't count on paint bombs flying through the air from nowhere. Or small children standing and staring from the pits of guiltiness.

"Aurelie Bonhoffen!" Mrs. Sneed's ruler-cut bangs shivered with rage.

Mrs. Sneed was a tall, colorless woman, except for the splatter of red paint now on her dress, parts of her face, and tightly wound hair. Even her silhouette was harsh, a collection of strict and measured lines. She liked math, not children. Not those unpredictable, loud, opinionated, and now paint-throwing children.

"Yes?" Aurelie's bleary, sleep-deprived eyes winced.

Mrs. Sneed's eyes pinpointed Aurelie like a scientist zeroing in on a strain of bacteria she planned to wipe out. "Did you throw paint all over the brand-new dress I had specially sent from London?"

Aurelie looked at her, confused.

"Nothing to say for yourself, eh? No excuses that you children are so fond of? Come with me."

Mrs. Sneed cantered toward the entrance of the school office, sending specks of paint flea-jumping into the air as her skirt swished angrily like an out-of-control fly swatter. Aurelie tried to keep up with small, skipping steps, but stopped when she passed the bush that hid the three boys. Her eyes rustled through the branches and made out the faces of her classmates staring back at her.

Sniggard did nothing to cover his smirk at how a plan that had gone so wrong had now become so perfectly right. He threw her a look, daring her to betray them. Charles poked out his tongue. But when she looked at Rufus, he quickly lowered the slingshot and recoiled as his finger caught on a thorn. He looked cornered, pinned down by the branches.

"Aurelie Bonhoffen!" Mrs. Sneed had gained ground in her indignant march. "When I give an order I expect it to be carried out."

Aurelie didn't move. Rufus stared back, knowing they were done for.

"It's—" Aurelie began.

"Enough! I'm not interested in words." Mrs. Sneed's face had turned as red as the spots on her dress. "I'm interested only in you . . . coming here . . . *now*."

The smile on Sniggard's lips rose even higher.

Aurelie gave one last look before she turned away and did as she was told.

Principal Farnhumple stood at the back of the room, polishing a souvenir spoon from Blackpool. She held it up to her face and saw herself reflected in its shiny surface before laying it neatly in a velvet box alongside spoons from other famous places: Big Ben, Brighton, Buckingham Palace. She usually polished them from A to Z and was unhappy about the interruption while she was only at B.

She turned and sat at her desk that was weighed down with two stained-glass lamps, a boxed collection of elegant pens, and a carved wooden beetle, to which she gave a small pat.

"Well? Are you going to answer me?"

Aurelie could feel the lateness of the night before sit heavily on her eyes. It was obvious from Mrs. Farnhumple's rouge-colored cheeks that she had asked a question, probably some time ago.

Aurelie tried hard to stifle a yawn. "Yes, miss."

Her head was a fog of fire-twirling, trapeze swinging, Black Forest cake, and cloudberry juice.

And, of course, the news about the Bonhoffen secret.

Aurelie remembered an old and crooked aunt she and Lilliana had visited in a castle overlooking the Baltic Sea in Estonia. The aunt moved around the castle without a sound, like a whisper of air, as if at any moment she would disappear. Lilliana explained that it was a broken heart and a son who had gone missing that caused her quiet footsteps. But Aurelie now wondered if this slumped and saddened woman was a ghost. Or a half-ghost. What did someone look like who had come back? Like this old woman? Maybe she'd come back because of her missing son. To search for him. To . . .

"It's *Mrs.* Farnhumple. It's very easy to remember. Why does everyone . . ." Mrs. Farnhumple looked away. Her husband was an entomologist, an expert on insects, and had been in the depths of the Amazon jungle studying the little creatures for the last five years. Some people said he found insects more appealing than his wife.

"What I am finding hard to understand," she said as she recomposed herself, "is that you seem to go out of your way to draw attention to yourself. Your teachers say you often stare into space and at times say the most inappropriate things. You told Mrs. Crankshaw that one of your favorite moments is when you get to be the back end of a cow."

Aurelie smiled. "Especially when Rolo is in the front. We make a very convincing cow when we're together."

Mrs. Farnhumple frowned.

"In the big top. During performances." Aurelie could tell her explanation was doing nothing to clear things up. "Miss Miel says I have a lively and curious mind, and that it's good to—"

"Miss Miel"—Mrs. Farnhumple's lip curled upward—"is young and has a lot to learn about educating children. I am more concerned about the comments of the *experienced* teachers, and the peculiar way you answer some of their questions."

Aurelie wilted under Mrs. Farnhumple's glare. "Sometimes I don't seem to give them the answers they want."

"It's not a matter of giving them answers they *want*, it's a matter of giving them answers that are *right*."

Mrs. Farnhumple leaned forward over her desk and clasped her spiderlike hands in front of her. "It is not just *any* child who is offered a place at such a fine school as Gribblesea Academy. A place, I need not remind you, that should be treated with respect and occupied by someone who is good enough to deserve it."

"Yes, Mrs. Farnhumple."

There was a heavy silence that left Aurelie unsure whether to leave, remain seated, or duck.

"Is everything all right at home, dear?" Mrs. Farnhumple asked almost gently.

"Huh?" Aurelie tilted her head and frowned.

"Not *huh*." Mrs. Farnhumple's left eye was beginning to twitch. "You mean *excuse me*. And sit up straight."

Aurelie lifted her body upright.

"Well, is it?" Her words were like hailstones. "Is everything all right at home?" she thundered.

"Yes, Mrs. Farnhumple."

Principal Farnhumple's wrinkles quivered so much that small avalanches of face powder stormed over the table.

"Things are perfectly . . ." Aurelie tried to stifle her yawn, but it came out in one noisy gush.

If Aurelie wasn't sure she'd upset Mrs. Farnhumple by then, she could be certain of it now. Her cheeks wobbled and turned purple, and her throat seized up so that she looked like a frill-necked lizard.

"I know this may not make much sense to you, but the responsibilities of a principal are many, the most important being to protect each child from moral corruption and the fall into delinquency." She stopped, as if this should have cleared up any confusion.

Aurelie blinked.

Principal Farnhumple snatched up a long black pen

and, for a frightening moment, Aurelie thought she might use her as a dartboard. She wrote something hurriedly, jamming the pen down and leaving deep grooves in the cream-colored paper.

"Give this to your parents when you get home."

Aurelie jumped as Mrs. Farnhumple slammed a rubber stamp onto the back of a school-crested envelope. It read: *From the principal, Mrs. Esmerelda Farnhumple.*

"You are excused." She may as well have said "You are a cockroach" for all the venom she crammed into it.

"Thank you, Mrs. Farnhumple." It seemed the right thing to say. Aurelie took the envelope and stood up. She had no idea what was inside, but it felt heavy with bad things to come.

Mr. Lucien B. Crook

Lucien B. Crook sniffed as he lifted his gold monocle and surveyed the view before him. It was a covetous, greedy sniff, punctuated by the smallest of grins on his red, fleshy lips. His black hair was waxed into a neatly coiffed wave and sat obediently beneath a stiff hat. He stood tall. Some might have described him as good-looking. His trim face was cleanly shaven except for a pencil-thin moustache drawing a neat line beneath his tapered nose.

In his long coat, immaculately pressed striped trousers, and vest of deep green, he slowly swept his monocle over the town. Past the far docks where hulking wooden cargo ships swayed and creaked in the calm of the bay. Over cobbled backstreets to his newspaper factory. Along the sweeping stretch of the high street, which was lined on one side with gleaming Georgian mansions and on the other by the rippling curve of the ocean.

When he spied the pier, he stopped.

The entrance was guarded by two wooden towers joined in the middle by a smoothly curved arch. In the center was a clock that had been ticking time for almost one hundred years. And above it all was a sign: GRIBBLESEA PIER.

Each letter stood over five feet tall, filled with lights that could be seen at night from the far edges of town.

Most of the pier buildings were a streaky gray-white, due to circling flocks of seagulls and pigeons. Inside were booths crammed with games of chance, stalls of rock candy, lollipops, and ice cream. There was the clash of bumper cars, the circling whirr of the Ferris wheel, and the rattle of the roller coaster that swung out over the sea.

Above each building and along the pier's side rails were strings of lace metalwork, which balanced rounded lights that glowed like miniature moons. Deck chairs sat open for passersby to stop and take in the smell of the sea or feel the warmth of the sun against their faces. To sit and listen and maybe even dream.

But Mr. Crook had no time for sitting, and he rarely dreamed.

He put his monocle away and was off.

His polished shoes clicked along the boardwalk as he passed brightly painted double doors where fishermen scaled their catch. Women sat in doorways chatting as they shelled prawns, shucked oysters, and turned whelks out of their snaillike shells.

Lucien B. Crook hurried past it all and only slowed when he reached the pier. He lifted one side of his lip in disgust at the curled ironwork gate, molded into images of crowns and lions, eaten away in places by rust. A crumbling lion's tail snapped off in his gloved hand. He let it fall to the ground with a "humph."

Crook strode through the crowd of running, chattering kids, past stalls of dolls and stuffed animals and the giant wave slide that sat quiet, its operator slumped and snoring into his crossed arms.

Lucien looked around at the faded signs offering henna tattoos, waffles, and pinwheel lollipops. He pulled his jacket tighter across his chest and held a handkerchief to his nose, as if the rust and fadedness were a contagious disease.

He looked about sharply until he saw the sign he was looking for: OFFICE. It was tipped on an angle and sat above the door of an oddly shaped building that looked more like an upside-down ice-cream cone, with twists of red and blue spiraling down from its pointed top.

It used to be the Tower of Terror.

On the outside was a swirling wooden slide where

smaller children could wend their terrified way on burlap sacks to the pit of rubber balls at the bottom. But
that was before Argus had found a nest of woodworm
that had almost eaten through the boards, making the
slide as thin as toast.

The balls had been removed and the slide closed,
too expensive to fix with all the other repairs. *Besides,*
Argus thought optimistically, *I've always wanted my
own office.*

Lucien knocked on the door. He heard the slow drawl
of a chair against the wooden floor. The door opened to
Argus's smile.

"Mr. Bonhoffen, I have come to make you an offer!"
Lucien said it with a bright-eyed grin, as though he was
offering the crown jewels.

Argus hoisted up his loose trousers. "Call me Argus,
and I guess you'd better come in."

Lucien took off his hat and walked into the twisted
building, which was strewn with books, posters of circus troupes, old wooden chairs with faded, lumpy cushions, and the damaged heads of laughing clowns.

"Please, sit down." Argus pulled a chair into the
center of the room. On his desk, along with accounting
books and papers, Lucien noticed a large pile of overdue
bills.

And a plastic skeleton.

"Sorry about him." Argus laid the skeleton on a

bench. "Normally he flies out in the ghost train, but his head fell off and it's on my list of things to fix."

Lucien wiped the chair with a handkerchief and turned the leering face of a clown away from him. "I would like to do business with you."

"I am always open to doing business," Argus replied. "But first, tea." He stepped toward a small gas stove and picked up a colorfully painted pot. "I can promise you this is the finest tea you will ever taste. Hand-grown and picked in a secret mountain location."

Lucien scowled. He liked to decide the way he did business, the way meetings would run, but here was this man offering *tea*.

Argus handed Lucien a steaming cup. "See what you make of that."

As soon as Lucien sipped, he knew in his toes that he'd tasted something special, something rare that left him with a slightly . . . elevated feeling.

Argus smiled. "I knew you'd like it. Haven't met a person yet who doesn't." He sipped. "What can I do for you, Mr. Crook?"

Lucien appeared to have momentarily lost his thoughts. He lowered his cup. "I'd like to offer you a substantial sum for your pier."

"I'm sorry?"

"A substantial sum, money, a free ticket out of the world of debt and worry."

"I'm not sure what to say."

Crook held up his hand. "Oh, don't thank me, I—"

"No, I mean, the pier is not for sale."

Crook was thrown. Briefly. "It's not for sale now," he resumed, "but only because you do not know the full extent of what I am offering. Think about it, Mr. Bonhoffen—"

"It's Argus."

"Argus." Lucien smiled. "The pier is very special to this town, but the costs of repair and maintenance, the wages, the upkeep . . . the money left over for you and your family must be a pittance. And on top of that, there are taxes that bite at our heels, never letting us move forward, always dragging us back into the dark world of . . ." he whispered, as if he was saying a dirty word, "debt."

Argus felt a dull pain in his chest. It had been there often and lately had been keeping him awake until dawn.

Lucien lifted his head. "We all need, at times, to do things which are difficult, or may even cause uneasiness, but we do it for the greater good, for progress, for . . ." Lucien winced at what he was about to say, but it had worked in other business transactions so he decided to use it again today. "For love."

He paused to let the word take its full effect.

"Imagine. The money I am offering you will enable you to buy a fine house, perhaps on a green, rolling hill that drifts down to the sea. Land enough for some chickens, a cow, even some goats. You could live the rest of your days watching your children and grandchildren from the veranda, knowing that it was *you* who made that once wise decision to remove them from a business that was in its last days, but one that had brought joy to the hearts of thousands in the glorious years it had been the pride of this town."

Argus stared through a window to the pier.

"What do you think?" Lucien's eyebrows rose with a flourish.

"What will you do with it?" Argus asked.

"Make it greater than it ever was," Lucien said with a flick of his hand.

"It would be nice for it to be made great again," Argus said quietly. "I will talk to my family."

Crook inhaled. "You will see. What I am offering makes sense. It is reason, it is fate, it is progress."

He shook Argus's hand. Argus took it back, cradling it as if it had been burned.

"I'll look forward to your answer." Lucien handed over a card. "You'll see my offer on the back. I always find it so uncouth to mention large sums of money out loud." He stood up. "Good day, Mr. Bonhoffen."

Once outside and with the door closed behind him, Lucien's broad smile collapsed into an irritated sneer. He firmly secured his hat and lifted his handkerchief to his nose.

With clipped and determined steps, punctuated by the snap of his cane, he hastily made his way off the pier.

The Family Meeting

In her room above the ghost train, Aurelie sat on her birthday chair. A breeze floated in through her skylight that opened onto a full moon. Light spilled everywhere: over her books, her shiny quilt, pillows, and the pier music box Rolo had made for her.

In her hands was Principal Farnhumple's sealed envelope. It would tell Argus and Amarella about the ruined dress, the insolence. It would tell them their daughter wasn't good enough. It would break their hearts.

But what could she do?

She stood from her chair, closed her bedroom door, and crept into the night to Argus's office.

The lights were still on. He'd been working late for weeks. When she moved closer, she heard voices and circled around the side of the building until she found a slightly opened window. She upturned a wastebasket, climbed on top, and poked her head up just high enough to see her family's serious faces.

"It is a good offer," Uncle Rindolf reasoned. "Enough to resettle in a smaller town, with smaller expenses. Start again, perhaps."

"Why start again when all we want is already here?" Lilliana asked.

"Because sometimes I think the only thing keeping the pier afloat are the barnacles," Argus joked.

No one laughed.

Aurelie frowned. Argus looked tired, as if someone had found a secret valve and let the air out of him.

Lilliana softened her voice. "Thoughts like that only make people sink, and we're not the sinking kind. How bad is it?"

"It's not good." Argus shook his head.

"Then together we'll work out a way to make it better. We've done it before, we'll do it again, you'll see."

Aurelie watched as Argus rubbed his forehead. "Each month there are new debts. If we accept Crook's offer now, we have a chance to set up somewhere else. If having this family provided for means giving up the pier, maybe it's the best thing we can do."

Amarella reached for Argus's hand.

"But what would we do?" Rolo asked. "I scare people, throw knives, fix rides, and play the trombone. That's all I know."

"We could learn new trades, perhaps." Rindolf shrugged.

"We can't leave," Lilliana said.

"Leave?" Aurelie whispered.

"Staying may mean our ruin," Argus said.

"There will be no ruin." Lilliana smiled. "Generations of Bonhoffens have worked hard on this pier. The spirit of each one of them fills every splinter of wood, and we owe it to them and us to keep it going."

"But everything has its time," Argus replied.

"This pier has been in our bones too long for us to give it away now," Lilliana said. "It would be like giving away the thing that makes you breathe. The very thing that keeps you alive. Without the pier, we would be nothing."

Argus's head fell forward—just a little. Enough for everyone to miss, except Aurelie. She'd never seen him like this. Or maybe she just hadn't noticed, hadn't looked closely enough.

"You can't leave the thing that makes you breathe." Rolo leaned back in his chair. "Even a simple man knows that." He sat forward again. "Sorry, Argus," he said quickly. "I didn't mean you are . . . I meant . . ." He wrenched his hands in his lap and lowered his voice. "You have my support, Argus. You always will."

"So we reject the offer?"

Everyone nodded.

Argus looked away toward the window. Aurelie jolted out of sight, until she realized he couldn't see her. He was staring at his own reflection in the glare of the windowpane. She wanted to touch his face. He'd once told her a single touch of a hand could melt rivers and hearts alike, could make men want to climb mountains or lead revolutions.

Just a touch.

"I will tell Mr. Crook of our decision," Argus said.

Aurelie stepped down from the wastebasket and folded Mrs. Farnhumple's letter into her pocket. She stepped away from the office and walked past the amusement arcade with its painted castle façade. She noticed the flags were frayed. One of the turrets had been worn through and was now home for a family of pigeons. Her eyes drifted to the merry-go-round. The noses of the horses were chipped, and so were their bellies where shoes had kicked into them from the stirrups. By the entrance to the Hall of Mirrors, the statue of the laughing man with his wobbling belly-o-jelly was so faded that his lips were the same color as his face.

Aurelie clasped the star ruby in her pocket.

The door of the office opened behind her and she slipped out of the light, hugging the shadows until she made it back to her room.

Principal Farnhumple

The limousine pulled away from the curb, leaving Rufus Bog struggling with a large backpack, a sports bag, and an oversize lunch box.

"Need a hand?" Aurelie asked from inside the fence.

"No," Rufus puffed. "I'm okay."

As he walked through the gate, his school jacket caught on the latch and his lunch box jerked out of his hand, spilling two bulky sandwiches, two apples, a banana, and a piece of chocolate cake.

Aurelie bent down and helped him pick them up, except for the cake that had crumbled into a chocolaty mess.

"Thanks," Rufus said into his shirt.

"You're late."

"I had a dentist's appointment. Mom wants me to get braces."

Aurelie bent her head and stared into his mouth. "But your teeth are really straight."

Rufus kept his lips close together. "Mom thinks they can be straighter. What are you doing here? School's already started."

"Juggling stones."

"Juggling stones?"

"Enzo says you need to practice whenever you can, so you don't get rusty." Aurelie sighed. "But mostly I'm waiting for my uncles."

"Why?"

"Principal Farnhumple wants to see my family. She thinks I'm 'in danger of moral corruption.'"

"Moral corruption?"

"Because of the balloon incident."

Rufus's head hung low. "I'm sorry about—"

"It's okay. You didn't do it."

"But I did."

Aurelie smiled. "I mean you wouldn't have done it if you hadn't let those boys talk you into it."

Rufus frowned. "They didn't talk me into it."

"Okay then." Aurelie shrugged. "If you say so."

"Aurelie!" Rindolf and Rolo hurried toward the school gate. They'd worn their best suits and hats, and even put fresh daisies in their lapels.

"Sorry we're late," Rindolf puffed. "Genius here

thought it'd be quicker to take the backstreets and—who would have known?—we got lost."

"Not lost," Rolo breathed. "We just went a little astray."

"Astray?" Rindolf shook his head. "So if we ended up in Siberia, would you say that we went *a little bit missing*?"

Rolo refused to answer and instead looked to the boy standing near Aurelie. "And who's this young man?"

"Rufus." Aurelie smiled. "He's a friend."

"We're Aurelie's uncles. I'm Rolo and he's Rindolf, and we—"

Aurelie grabbed Rolo's hand. "Are late for the meeting."

"Yes, of course."

They hurried toward the office. Rolo straightened his tie. "Do I look okay?"

"All the office ladies will be throwing themselves at you." Aurelie kissed his cheek.

"Or running for cover." Rindolf smirked. "Come on, handsome."

Aurelie turned to see Rufus hadn't moved; she waved. He gave an uncertain wave back.

They climbed the stone steps of the main school building and rushed down the dead-straight corridors, which were lined with gloomy portraits of dusty principals and grim-faced Academy trustees.

Behind a glass sliding window, an office lady with a

nest of perfect curls piled on her head raised a curious eyebrow. Her eyes ran down the length of the two men in the same way they might have if a mangy hound had tracked mud through her house.

"You must be the Bonhoffens." Her eyes flicked to the clock on the wall. "Please sign here." The assistant placed a pen on the register and whispered into her telephone receiver. After Rolo and Rindolf had signed in, she slid carefully past them and knocked on the principal's door.

"Come in," a voice intoned.

The assistant opened the door onto Mrs. Farnhumple perched behind her wide desk. She finished a letter with a flourish and looked up. Her momentarily smiling face nose-dived into an agitated scowl. "Aurelie, can I see you for a moment? Outside."

"Yes, Mrs. Farnhumple."

"Please sit down, um . . ."

"I'm Rindolf and he's Rolo." Rindolf held his hat to his chest so tightly he almost crushed it.

Mrs. Farnhumple looked as if she had a bad case of indigestion. "Quite. Well." She clutched her stomach. "Please sit down, Mr. Rindolf and Mr. Rolo." She motioned toward two seats opposite her desk. "We won't be long."

Mrs. Farnhumple stared at the doorknob long

enough for Aurelie to realize she was waiting for her to open it. Aurelie leaped at the door, turned the knob, and followed Mrs. Farnhumple outside.

"Where are your parents?"

"My parents?"

Mrs. Farnhumple eyed her with a look edged with frost. "Your parents. Your mother and father. The ones that look after you and send you to school. The ones I asked to see."

Aurelie thought about her answer carefully, but no matter how much she tried to think of one the principal would like, she knew it would come out wrong.

"You mean . . . Argus and Amarella?"

"You call your parents by their first names?"

Aurelie needed to get the sour expression off Mrs. Farnhumple's face. "There are lots of people who look after me. Not just Argus . . . I mean my father and mother." She smiled. "Lilliana always says, 'Why settle for one set of parents when you can have many?'"

"Lilliana?"

"My grandmother."

What followed next was the kind of quiet that preceded something bad happening. When someone is about to get it.

Mrs. Farnhumple's eyes squinted. "You can't have more than one set of parents. That . . . is . . . ridiculous."

"Yes, Mrs. Farnhumple."

Mrs. Farnhumple's eyebrows shot up. "Who's inside my office then?"

"Uncle Rindolf and Uncle Rolo."

"Uncles, eh? Well, I guess my only choice is to talk to them."

Her hand wrenched the doorknob as if she wanted to pull it off.

"Ah, gentlemen, sorry to keep you waiting." She was suddenly all smiles and ballet steps as she danced to her seat. Aurelie stood beside her uncles. "This is a highly unusual situation. Usually when I ask to see the parents of a student, it's the mother and father who keep the appointment."

"They're busy. Lots to do back at the pier. Plus"— Rolo winked at his niece—"we don't mind one bit."

"We're always here for Aurelie," Rindolf added.

Mrs. Farnhumple smiled through tightened lips. "The reason I asked you here today is that I'm very concerned about Aurelie."

Rolo's face creased. "She's okay, isn't she? There's nothing wrong with her, is there?" He placed his hand against his niece's forehead.

"No, not physically wrong, Mr. Rolo, but she's not as she should be." Mrs. Farnhumple took a large file out of her top drawer. "Here at Gribblesea Academy, we like to take a special interest in each child. To see that they

learn the essentials for becoming good, honest, up-
standing human beings."

"That's our Aurelie, all right," Rindolf said proudly
as he squeezed his hat out of shape even more.

"Yes." Mrs. Farnhumple paused. "Certainly. You see,
the thing is, Aurelie isn't quite like the other children."

"Thank you." Uncle Rolo adjusted his tie and smiled.

"I don't necessarily mean that in a *good* way, Mr. Rolo."

"Oh," Rolo said.

"Best if we just listen, I think." Uncle Rindolf shivered a little in the dark, mud-colored office. His nose
twitched from the dust that had settled into the rows of
papers, cluttered shelves, and thick, musty curtains. Being
surrounded by so much dust and darkness gave Rindolf
the eerie feeling of being buried alive.

"For instance, it is absolutely inexcusable that a student would throw a paint balloon at a teacher."

"Oh, that." Rindolf smiled. "Aurelie told us. It's all
fine, though. She said she didn't do it."

"Of course she did."

Rindolf frowned.

"There were no other children around except Aurelie. No one else could possibly have done it. But that's
not all. I have been wanting to talk to Aurelie's family
for some time. She doesn't seem to have the same idea
about things as the other children." Mrs. Farnhumple
paused. "In dress, for example."

Aurelie dropped her eyes to her lap and the cut-up patchwork of materials that made up her skirt. Lilliana had sewn them together out of old costumes and favorite dresses she used to wear when she was young.

"Excuse me for asking, Mrs. Farnhumple." Rindolf leaned his head to one side. "But what does the way someone dresses have to do with anything?"

Mrs. Farnhumple's mouth opened and closed as if she was gasping for breath. "It has everything to do with everything. It's how the world sees you, it's respect, it's manners, it's the very fabric of how our society functions."

Rindolf scowled and scratched his head. Mrs. Farnhumple stood up and continued, as if she was conducting some kind of invisible orchestra.

"The school community is like the world community. There are rules and ways of behaving that students need to follow if they are going to succeed in life and make something of themselves. It is a great privilege to be a member of our community, but if Aurelie is to remain at our school, we need to see—"

A great crash erupted. Mrs. Farnhumple spun around to see Rindolf and Aurelie helping Rolo to his feet.

"Is everything all right, Mr. Rolo?"

"Yes, I . . . I seem to have fallen off my chair. Please, go on."

Aurelie stifled a giggle as she resumed standing beside her uncles.

"If Aurelie is to remain at our school, we need to see an improvement."

"Improvement?" Rindolf asked.

"Yes, in her dress, her attitude, her behavior. We can't have children throwing paint bombs at teachers, otherwise, in just a few years, civilization will be in a terrible state."

"Yes, but she didn't throw—" Rolo began, but Rindolf placed a hand on his brother's arm and silenced him.

"As her punishment, she is to write an essay on why teachers deserve the utmost respect, along with a formal apology for poor Mrs. Sneed. Aurelie will, of course, pay for a new dress."

Aurelie looked up. "But Miss Farnhumple, I didn't—"

"Mrs. It's *Mrs.* Farnhumple."

She handed Rindolf the bill. His face whitened. "Dresses are expensive these days."

"Maybe Aurelie will think of that before she does anything like it again." Mrs. Farnhumple stood. "I'll expect the essay, apology, and payment by the week's end. Aurelie is excused from school, and we look forward to seeing her tomorrow to start afresh."

Rolo, Rindolf, and Aurelie made their way outside and passed the assistant, who buried her head behind piles of papers as they went by.

It wasn't until they were sitting on the pebbles of Gribblesea Beach that they spoke.

"Did that make sense to anyone else?" Rolo threw up his hands.

"Some of it," Rindolf said.

"Which parts?"

"The part where . . . where . . ." Rindolf shook his head. "No. None of it."

"Well, don't be saying things make sense when they don't."

"I thought maybe just a little of it did, but—"

"I don't want to let Argus and Amarella down," Aurelie interrupted.

The two brothers swapped looks before firmly sandwiching their niece between them. "How could you possibly do that?" Rolo asked.

"In fact, I think that is a distinct impossibility." Rindolf nodded.

"A preposterosity."

Aurelie smiled. "That's not a word."

Rolo threw his head back. "It is now."

"When it comes to being proud of you, Aurelie Bonhoffen," Rindolf said, "your parents wouldn't know how to be prouder."

"And they're very smart people." Rolo wriggled into her. "Nearly as smart as us, and we think you're perfect."

Aurelie laughed.

"What's not to be proud of?" Rindolf threw out his arms. "You know how to scare the dickens out of people, how to fix a broken bumper car, how to juggle fire . . . and you can add up numbers in your head as quickly as anybody I know."

"You can name the capital of any country in the world," Rolo added. "And you've known how to read since you could sit up and hold a book. Before then even."

Aurelie paused. "I know about the ghosts too."

"Ah, that," Rindolf said. "That takes getting used to. You just have to remember that each family has their own something that makes them special, and that's ours. It's hard to understand at first, but it gets easier."

Rolo picked up a pebble and tossed it back and forth in his hands. "It doesn't happen very often, but Rindolf's right. You'll see. One day you might even find it comes in handy."

"Unlike your uncle Rolo. We're still waiting for him to come in handy." Rindolf laughed until Rolo's pebble bounced off his head. "Ouch!"

"The only thing you're really handy with is that overworking mouth of yours."

"Is that so? Well—"

"Please don't tell Argus about today," Aurelie said. "I'll find a way to pay for the dress without bothering him."

"What happened today stays between us," Rindolf said. "And Rolo and I will pay for the dress."

"I don't care what Mrs. Farnhumple has to say."

65

Rolo flicked his head. "If it means changing one thing about you, I won't have it!"

"Neither will I." Rindolf straightened.

"Are all your teachers like her?" Rolo scowled.

"No. Most of them are really nice."

"That's a relief. I think I'd rather eat my hat than sit in class with too many of her." He held up his very crumpled hat.

"Looks like someone's already started," his brother said.

Aurelie laughed.

Rindolf caught a glimpse of the pier clock. "Lilliana's going to do a lot worse to us if we don't get the ghost train prepared for tonight. Race you to the gates."

Rolo grabbed Rindolf's jacket and pulled him onto the stones.

"Not lying down you won't. Ha." Rindolf flung his leg out just in time to trip him up. "Oooph!"

"Why you—" Rolo began.

"See you there," Aurelie yelled over her shoulder.

"Looks like we're on," Rolo said.

The two brothers picked themselves up from the pebbles and raced after Aurelie to the pier.

Mayor Finnigus Bog

Mayor Finnigus Bog wasn't a thin man and, in fact, he'd been called, in not-so-polite circles, pudgy, rotund, even chubby. Some said he had been worn into shortness by the controlling nature of his wife. Others said it was because his pockets were heavy from the weight of too much money.

Each morning he would stand before his polished, freestanding mirror and offer a kind and welcoming smile. "There you are, Finnigus Bog. You're a handsome devil, aren't you?"

He examined his smile first, then maneuvered his face into expressions he might need later in the course of the business day: stern but charitable, harsh but fair, understanding to a limit. His favorite look he kept until last, the look that offered others the promise of great things—a vacation, a pay raise, time off for a wedding . . . but only a hint of a promise. A promise left no room to wiggle out if the deal didn't serve him well. He had a special look for that. A slight downward turn of the lip that said, *Sometimes life doesn't turn out how we would have hoped.*

His smile faltered. "Indeed," he said quietly.

He stood taller and tucked his stomach in. If he stood far enough away from the mirror and squinted, his profile became the figure of a strapping young man, not the portly midriff of a middle-aged one. He still cut a fine figure for the sculptor who was chiseling his likeness into a marble statue for generations of Gribblesea citizens to admire. He imagined it now, standing over six and a half feet tall with an inscription in a brass plaque that would say:

TO THIS MEASURE OF GREATNESS, WE OWE SO MUCH.

At the sound of a car door slamming outside, his stomach bulged out again in an abrupt exhale. It was a particular car door slam—an expensive one he'd have recognized through a hailstorm—and it came from the back lane of Mayor Bog's house.

"He's early," Bog complained. "How's a man to do business before breakfast?"

He fixed his tie, slipped into his jacket, and hurried down the stairs to the corridor, where he promptly tripped over a pair of young legs.

"What in the . . . ?" He regained his footing.

"Sorry, Father." Rufus, the owner of the outstretched legs, whipped them in and sat up.

"You don't think there would be a better place to play with toys?"

"It's not a toy, sir. I'm making a model of the *Mary Rose*. A ship that—"

Mayor Bog heard a thump on the back door. "Play in your toy room. I've an important guest."

Rufus watched his father almost run to the door. "A ship that Henry the Eighth built." He moved into the room.

"Why, Mr. Crook." Mayor Bog almost bowed. "How nice to—"

"Not here, Bog," he snapped through a hardened jaw. "Let's be a *little* discreet."

Crook charged into the house and down a hallway decorated with expensive rugs, fine art, and priceless vases before climbing the spiral staircase to Bog's study. He made himself comfortable in a deep leather sofa while Bog panted and hurried to the chair behind his desk.

"Are you well, Mr. Crook?"

"I've had a particularly annoying morning evicting a family from one of my apartments. They'd failed to pay the last two weeks' rent. One of the little runts even slobbered on my leg." He pulled a hanky from his pocket and wiped his trousers. "So I'm hoping my bad day's about to change. How is everything going with *you*?"

"Very well, thank you, apart from a slight backache after a game of tennis I—"

"I don't mean with you personally," Crook cut in, scissor-sharp. "I mean with the *pier*."

"Yes, of course." The mayor apologized. "The increased taxes are having an effect: fireworks tax, permission-to-operate-after-five-p.m. tax, a noise tax. The Bonhoffens are turning out to be more resilient than we thought. But I'm sure it won't be long now."

"How long?"

"Perhaps . . ." Mayor Bog paused, desperate to find the right answer. "Three months."

"Three months! I must have it before then."

Mayor Bog straightened. "There is a fondness for the pier even though it is old, Mr. Crook. You *are* going to keep it as a pier, like you said?"

"Absolutely." Crook's smile blossomed. "Only more elegant and refined than it is now." He sprang to his feet and swung Bog's chair around to face the pier in the distance. "It will be restored to all its former glory. Imagine." Crook swept his hand before them. "Instead of a crumbling eyesore, the pier will be painted and repaired, spruced and polished so that it shines once again as the jewel of Gribblesea." Bog felt Crook's breath against his cheek. "And the whole town would have you to thank for it. Hence, that very handsome donation to fund the completion of the statue in your honor."

Crook leaped forward, threw open the window, and breathed in deeply. "Smell that."

Bog sniffed.

"Can you smell it?"

Bog nodded. "Yes?"

"That is the smell of success." Crook latched onto Bog's shoulders. "*Your* success. And all you have to do is get rid of that family."

"What if"—Bog had an idea—"once the pier is restored, the Bonhoffens are employed to run it?"

"Run it?" Crook's hands fell from Bog's shoulders. "Run all our hard work into the ground, more like. The Bonhoffens once did a fine job, but their ways are old and the pier would once again be led into the sorry state it's in now. I applaud them—we all do—but it is time for them to take their final bow."

Crook strode to the door. "I expect them out of there by the end of the month."

Bog's lips quivered. "But that's only—"

"Two weeks. Yes." Crook's smile was wide and unflinching. "How *is* the statue coming along?"

"The marble is in position and the sculptor has made great progress. It should be ready in weeks."

"Excellent. A time when we shall all get what we want," Crook said. "I'll see myself out." His leather shoes clacked against the polished floorboards, like a clock counting down the time Bog had left.

The mayor sat heavily in his chair. His head fell forward into his hands.

He stayed like this for several moments before he chose a pen from his drawer and began to write. From afar his concentration could have looked like a man writing a love letter or a note to a dear friend. But he was writing no such thing. It was a list. A list that went like this:

1. More taxes . . . an entertainment tax? A close-to-the-sea tax? Not enough time.
2. Spread rumors that the pier is unsafe and likely to fall into the sea at any moment? Too slow. A newspaper article would be faster? Journalists to be trusted? None.
3. Eviction under the Health Regulations Act. Excess of mold, mildew, damp, etc.
4. Sabotage—make the pier condemnable . . . Lice? Termites? Other vermin infestation. Rats?

Mayor Bog lifted his head.

"No respectable citizen would stand the filth of a plague of rats where innocent children play." He sat back in his chair. "You are good, Finnigus."

His pen scribbled across the page, outlining further details of his plan, when he was interrupted.

"Mayor Bog? Is it okay for me to come in?"

A thin wisp of a teenager in an oversize suit that dripped off his shoulders poked his head around the door.

"Speaking of unwanted pests," Mayor Bog murmured before erupting into a sugar-sweet smile. "I'd say you're already in, wouldn't you, Julius?"

"I guess." Julius kept standing where he was.

"Well, come in!"

The boy was the son of a cousin and, having failed miserably at every job he'd ever put his hand to, Bog had agreed to give him a position at the council and somehow teach him how to do it well. "And sit down."

Julius, in his hurry to sit, tripped over his own shoes and landed face-first in a rack of coats before pulling himself out and sitting in the chair opposite.

Mayor Bog let out a long, drawn-out, *why me?* sigh. "The town of Gribblesea is in danger."

"Danger, sir?"

"Yes, in danger of losing its fine and noble reputation because of a blight, a stain, a blemish that is threatening to bring our beloved town's name into disrepute."

"Disrepute, Mayor Bog?" The boy teetered on the edge of his chair. "What is it, sir?"

Mayor Bog stood slowly and looked out the window. "It's . . . the pier."

"The pier?" Julius laughed. "But everyone loves the

pier. It has rides and cotton candy and waffles and the ghost train. I love the ghost train. Why, only last week I—"

"Yes, yes." Mayor Bog cut Julius off before the trip down memory lane gave him a headache. "It was once a place to be proud of, but it is old now—its glory dimmed—and the maintenance costs are far too much for the Bonhoffens. We can't all keep having fun at the expense of a family who has given so much to this town."

"No, sir." Julius's face was a portrait of guilt.

"It is unfair to leave these good people with the crippling expenses of upkeep and wages and taxes when they simply can't afford it."

Julius frowned. "But aren't we responsible for the taxes that—"

"Stay focused, Julius," Bog sneered. "These are good people who are suffering under the weight of a business that is threatening to drown them, and it is our duty to save them."

Julius brightened. "Maybe the council can give the Bonhoffens money, for restoration and upkeep. That is what we do with the parks and roads and the governor's residence and your car and your wife's tennis lessons and—"

"Shush! Shush! Shush!"

The force of the mayor's words pushed the nephew into the back of his seat.

"If we gave money to everyone who got themselves into financial strife, we'd have nothing left to run the town."

"Yes, Mayor. Of course."

"No, Julius, we have to accept that the pier needs new management and fresh ideas to restore it to its former glory and save the fine reputation of Gribblesea."

Julius felt a stirring of love for his town in his stomach. Or was it that he hadn't had breakfast?

"The problem is, Julius, the pier isn't just in need of restoration. I've had reports that it is unstable and may even be"—Mayor Bog screwed up his face—"infested with vermin."

"Vermin, sir?"

"Yes." Mayor Bog put on his look of careful concern. "And we simply cannot stand by while our fine town is sullied. We must encourage the Bonhoffens to leave so that a new era can begin."

He placed his hand on the boy's shoulder. The nephew shifted slightly.

"If only we knew how to do it." Mayor Bog paced the room, his eyes darting to Julius, whose face, unfortunately, seemed as full of ideas as a rather small rock. "If there were rats on the pier, for example, a lot of them, then the Health Department could be called in and the pier closed. We could announce the new owners and the restoration could commence immediately."

"So the Bonhoffens would be replaced? Just like that?"

"Not 'just like that.' They would be paid a large sum by the new owners and be given the chance to live free from the worry of debt. They could be happy knowing that generations of Bonhoffens have brought this town such joy. What could make them happier?"

"So, to make them happy you need rats on the pier?"

"Yes."

"If we were to let rats loose on the pier, everyone's problems would be solved?"

Mayor Bog turned to the boy. "I think you may have something there, but how could we do that?"

"I know a man who can supply me with all the rats we'll need. He runs a snake farm and breeds them for the snakes to eat."

Mayor Bog raised an eyebrow. "Well done, lad. I think you may have just rescued the reputation of Gribblesea." Julius blushed from the unusual praise. "How soon can you make it happen?"

"I'll arrange it immediately." Julius headed for the door before slowing. "Sir? Are you sure releasing rats on the pier is in the best interests of Gribblesea?"

"Not only is it in the town's best interests, it would be a *crime* for us to let this poor family suffer any longer."

Aurelie's Announcement

Aurelie stood outside Argus's office. She took a deep breath and lifted her foot to the first step. A broad figure swung open the door before closing it softly behind him.

"Enzo?"

Enzo stopped, a wad of money in his hand. His face reddened and his eyes blinked fast.

"You're not usually up this early," Aurelie said.

His hand crept to his pocket and sneaked the money inside. "No," Enzo replied. "It's an unusual day." He sat on the top step and patted the spot next to him. Aurelie sat beside his bulky frame.

"Are you leaving?"

"Yes," he whispered. "We've had an offer to perform in Canada." He looked down. "It's a very good offer."

"When do you leave?"

"Today."

"But you never mentioned anything at practice yesterday."

"We made up our minds quickly. Thought it better to leave right away." His fingers twisted between his knees. "Promise you'll think of me each time you twirl fire." He held a warning finger close to her nose. "And never show off—that's when people get hurt."

Aurelie nodded, a sharp pain in her throat. "Will you come back to visit?"

"Every time I can." Enzo pulled up his sleeve and flexed an arm. "Feel this." Aurelie grabbed his tattooed bicep. "Harder." Aurelie gripped with both hands. "Harder."

"That's as hard as I can."

"That's how strong the bond is between you and me, even when we are far apart. The star ruby will remind you of how strong you are. Even when you don't feel it."

Aurelie took it out of her pocket. "I carry it everywhere."

Enzo blinked a few times and folded her into his coat. His eyes shut tight. He gave her one last kiss on the forehead before walking onto the pier.

Aurelie wiped her sleeve across her face and swung open the office door.

"Are we going to lose the pier?"

"Ah, just what I needed, my little girl to bring me some sunshine." Argus sat at the table with Amarella. He pointed to his cheek. "And my morning kiss?"

Aurelie kissed her father. "And, no, the pier is ours for keeps."

"But Enzo's leaving." The sadness of it caught in Aurelie's throat in a gasp.

Amarella held Aurelie's face in her hands. "Enzo and his troupe have accepted an invitation to join a circus based in Montreal. It's a chance to perform all over the world, even as far away as Australia."

Amarella pulled out a chair. The table was laid out with plates, jams, and freshly made sweet breads. She poured Aurelie a glass of cloudberry juice.

Aurelie sat. "Is anyone else leaving?"

"No. Enzo had a good offer, that's all." Argus dished out spoonfuls of porridge, sweetened with Lilliana's cranberry syrup. "And there isn't a finer breakfast than this to get you ready for school."

Aurelie turned the spoon in her hand. "I'm not going to school."

Amarella felt her daughter's cheeks and forehead. "Do you feel sick?"

"No." It was almost the truth.

"Has something happened?" Argus sat beside her.

"No. Nothing. I've decided it's better if I don't go back."

"Better for who?" Argus squared his shoulders toward his daughter.

"For everyone. I learn just as much here as I do at school. In fact, I probably learn more. I already borrow books from Lilliana, and I borrow lots of others from the public library. Rolo and Rindolf teach me about music and juggling and fixing things, and when I'm not doing any of that I could pull my weight a little more and—"

"What brought this on?" Argus asked.

"Nothing." Aurelie swirled the porridge in her bowl.

"Nothing?"

She blurted it out. "School's too expensive, and we can't afford it. We'd be better off spending the money on the pier."

"Would we?" He eyed her carefully.

"We thought you liked school," Amarella said.

"I do."

Argus stroked his daughter's head. "Amarella and I want to make sure you learn as much about the world as you can, so that you can be anyone you want to be, and school is one way to make that happen. So, unless there's some compelling reason you shouldn't go, like you're in danger of being eaten by a wild bear, then I guess that's that. Are there any wild bears I should know about?"

Aurelie smiled. "No."

"Do you want to be in school?"

"Yes."

Argus waved his spoon in the air. "Then everything's as it should be. Now, how's that porridge? It's one of Lilliana's best batches of cranberry, and you know how she'll be if she finds you didn't eat every last speck."

"I'll miss Enzo," Aurelie said.

Argus's smile had a touch of sadness in it. "We all will. But we're lucky—people like Enzo leave a big enough memory, so he'll never be forgotten."

Disaster at Sea

Who could have known such terrible tragedy was to strike this magnificent ship?"

Rufus Bog stood before his classmates with his model of the *Mary Rose* on a table beside him. He'd pointed out the features of the famous warship: the lower gun deck, the galley, the crew's quarters, and the crow's nest.

"The *Mary Rose* was one of King Henry the Eighth's favorite ships, and he described her as 'the fairest flower of all the ships that ever sailed.'"

Stifled giggles rose from Charles and Sniggard. Rufus looked up. His thoughts became muddled and his hands began to shake. He turned back to the *Mary Rose* and her cannons, decks, and sails, and resumed his report.

"She . . . she . . . was one of England's first ships built purposely for war. She had a long and successful career until July 19, 1545. King Henry the Eighth went to Southsea to watch his fleet set out to war against the French. She had more than ninety guns on her decks, and the English flag flew proudly overhead. But, instead of watching her sail off to glory, the king watched as the *Mary Rose* keeled over in a blast of wind and sank. Some claim there were up to seven hundred crew members, but only around thirty survived."

Rufus paused. "And the *Mary Rose*, along with all the hopes King Henry the Eighth held for her, was lost to the sea."

"Well done, Rufus, for a courageous and sad tale, and a masterfully built ship." Miss Miel led the applause.

"My fairest flower." Sniggard blew Rufus a kiss as he wound his way back to his desk. Rufus tripped over the leg of his chair. Sniggard and Charles giggled harder.

A few desks to his right, Rufus saw Aurelie. She smiled. With the eyes of Sniggard and Charles still on him, Rufus turned away.

"And for our next speaker we must step into the courtyard. Aurelie Bonhoffen has something very special to show us."

Aurelie opened her desk and grabbed a canvas bag. Before she closed it, she saw an envelope tucked between her books. As the class piled outside, she slipped a finger beneath the seal and found the envelope filled with money and a note. It read: For the dress.

She looked around the class to see if anyone was watching her, but most of them had already left.

"Ready, Aurelie?" Miss Miel smiled from the doorway. "I have the sand bucket ready for you as requested."

"Yes, Miss Miel." She slipped the envelope to the back of her desk.

In the courtyard, Aurelie began by juggling three balls. "No one can really say when juggling started, but we know it existed in ancient Egypt from a carving on the wall of a prince's tomb that shows female dancers throwing balls." She tossed the balls higher. "In the Middle Ages, some religious men linked juggling with low morals—even witchcraft—but I think it was more about people wanting to entertain. Some made it more exciting by juggling dangerous objects, like knives and fire. I learned to juggle from a man called Enzo. He was the lead fire-twirler at the pier and has performed for kings and princesses. He began teaching me when I was four. I started with soft balls, then I moved on to rings, clubs . . . and now this."

Aurelie put the balls back in her bag. She slipped on her gloves decorated with flames.

"What's with the gloves?" Sniggard said loud enough for Aurelie to hear.

"To protect my hands," she explained.

"From what?"

"From *this*." She took out a baton and lit both ends. The class gasped.

"There's no need to worry," Aurelie said. "As long as I respect the rules of fire-twirling, no one will get hurt."

Aurelie began with some simple twirling from one hand to the other. The fire dipped and curved before she threw the baton in the air, spinning above her. There were small cries of amazement as she spun around, reached up, and caught it overhead.

The class surged into a wave of clapping and cheering. Miss Miel winked at Aurelie, who smiled until she saw herself being mimicked by Charles and Sniggard.

Aurelie searched the class. "For this next part I need a volunteer." She pointed at Sniggard.

"I'm not being your volunteer."

Aurelie held her lit baton before her. "There's nothing to be afraid of."

"I'm not afraid."

"Good," Miss Miel answered. "Then you won't mind being Aurelie's volunteer. She has shown me what she can do. She's very safe."

Sniggard shuffled to the front, his hands clenched in his pockets.

"Stand very still," Aurelie instructed, "and you'll be fine."

Sniggard turned to the students, whose faces were a

mixture of grins and barely held back laughter. He kept his hands at his sides and waited.

Aurelie twirled the baton in one hand and then the other before swooping it around her body. She held Sniggard's glare and returned a calm smile. Sniggard swallowed hard and tried to steady his shuddering body.

All eyes focused on the flames.

Aurelie gave Sniggard one last grin before hurling the baton into the air, directly above him. He shut his eyes and let out a small whimper. Aurelie raced forward as the baton circled over Sniggard's head. She reached up and caught it just behind him.

The class applauded wildly.

Sniggard opened his eyes and spun around to see Aurelie extinguish the flame in a bucket beside her. He elbowed his way to the back of the class, eyeing a clapping Rufus and Charles, who went instantly quiet.

Clusters of questions fired at Aurelie. She answered each one carefully, just as Enzo had taught her. She looked up and met Rufus's eyes. For once he didn't look away.

After school, Aurelie headed for the Alleys—a labyrinth of winding, cobbled backstreets that lay between the sea and Gribblesea Academy. They bustled with fishmongers, greengrocers, bakers, and booksellers. Old women in shawls and hooped earrings sat at tables telling fortunes from the palm of a hand or a clump of soggy tea leaves. There were street performers with fiddles and accordions and harmonicas and dogs that danced in tiaras and tutus.

Aurelie wound her way through it all, ducking under trays of tarts, stepping through racks of silk scarves, until she found Sniggard, Charles, and Rufus sitting outside a cafe with three oversize milk shakes and chocolate fudge brownies. She blew a curl from her face, lifted her bag onto her shoulder, and headed toward them.

"Did you ask for extra malt in mine?" Sniggard complained.

"I asked," Rufus answered.

"Yeah, well, it doesn't taste like it." Sniggard took long, loud sips before looking up. "Well, who do we have here?" He wiped a line of froth from his mouth. "It's the Fire Girl."

"Fire Girl." Charles laughed.

"My name's Aurelie."

"What kind of a name's Aurelie?"

"It was my great-great-grandmother's name. It means 'golden.'"

"Golden?" Sniggard slapped Rufus's back. "Well, aren't you precious. What are you doing here, Golden Child?"

"I overheard you say you were coming here, and I wanted to—"

Sniggard slurped noisily. "Sorry, I can't hear you."

Charles laughed through a mouthful of brownie that flew into the air in crumbled specks.

Aurelie turned to Rufus. "I wanted to tell you that I liked your talk about the *Mary Rose*."

Charles and Sniggard looked at each other before exploding into monkeylike guffaws. "She liked your talk about that toy ship of yours," Sniggard cried. "What do you think of that, Rufus? Fire Girl thinks you're a genius. Next she'll be asking you to be her boyfriend."

Rufus's eyes flicked around the table.

"Well?" Charles asked. "What do you think of that?"

Sniggard's and Charles's eyes bore into him. "Thanks, but I don't need a compliment from the school freak."

"School freak." Charles slapped the table. "That's great."

Sniggard patted Rufus on the back and threw a sharp look at Aurelie, daring her to say more. She stood firm, making no attempt to move. "I thought it was good."

Sniggard grunted. "She's only sucking up to you because your dad's the mayor."

"Yeah," Charles snorted, "the mayor."

Aurelie waited until their laughter withered before turning away. Rufus concentrated on the swirl of thick, chocolaty bubbles and sipped, his eyes sneaking a glance at Aurelie's every step until she disappeared into the crowd.

A Crash in the Night

I thought I'd been abandoned." Lilliana added a pinch of cinnamon to a steaming pot of hot chocolate.

"Sorry," Aurelie said. "There was a problem with the ghost train, and the last one ended later than usual."

The smell of chocolate drifted through the air as Lilliana poured her brew into two large mugs. She spooned freshly whipped cream on top, followed by sprinkled flakes of chocolate.

"How did the fire-twirling go at school?"

"Good." Aurelie smiled. "Everyone loved it. Miss Miel said my research was very insightful."

"You didn't show off, I hope."

"No. It's Enzo's first rule." Aurelie's smile fell.

"Goodbyes are some of the hardest times we face. That chocolate won't fix it, but it'll help." Lilliana kissed Aurelie on the forehead and pointed to her bed. "Jump in."

Aurelie climbed into Lilliana's bed, which was stuffed

so full of feathers and covered with so many quilts that she felt as if she were floating. She took a sip. "One of your best yet."

Lilliana wiggled in close to Aurelie and sipped her own chocolate. "I think you're right." She nodded. "Rindolf and Rolo told me about the meeting with the principal."

"You won't say anything to Argus, will you?"

"Not if you don't want me to."

Aurelie warmed her hands around the mug. "Mrs. Farnhumple said I'm not like the other children."

Lilliana frowned. "And that's a problem?"

"She said that—"

"Are you happy being you?"

Aurelie shrugged. "Yes."

"Do you worry about not being like the others?"

"Not really. Miss Miel says everyone's unique, and if we were all the same the world would be boring."

"Miss Miel is a smart woman." Lilliana took a loud sip. "What else did your principal say?"

"She thinks I should dress more like the other kids."

"Why is she worrying about how you're dressed?" Lilliana's chocolate almost spilled from her mug. "That woman deserves a good shake to knock some sense into her."

"Lilliana!"

"Oh, I don't mean it . . . but you could let an old lady

have some fun thinking about it." She laughed. "We're all here, in our own way, adding something to the world no one else can. How is anyone going to do that when being the same is all they're concentrating on? Do the other kids give you a hard time?"

"Some, but most of them are really nice. The annoying ones seem to take up more room, but I can handle them."

Lilliana smiled. "I'm sure you can. Bonhoffens have made a whole family history out of being different. And made their mark doing it. Now, what else is worrying you? And don't say nothing 'cause I know something is."

Aurelie paused. "Do you think we're going to lose the pier?"

"Did those uncles of yours tell you that?"

"No. I heard you all talking at the family meeting."

Lilliana's hand brushed her granddaughter's cheek. "We're staying right where we are. There are a few money issues we need to sort out, but we've been through worse. Your job is to concentrate on school and not worry about the business or what other people think you should or shouldn't be." She held Aurelie's chin. "And remember, the best way to deal with people who say untrue things about you is to prove them wrong."

A muffled crash came from outside.

"Did you hear that?" Lilliana asked.

Aurelie nodded.

They slipped out from beneath the covers and kneeled before the window above the bed. Lilliana lifted a corner of the curtain. The pier lay in the misty light of the lampposts. The flags of the circus tent and the canvas covers of the rides fluttered and slapped.

"Must be the wind stirring things up."

"Or it could be Rolo." Aurelie spied her uncle walking in the shadows. His body hunched into the wind, his head bent low. "He's been sad lately."

"He has a heavy heart." Lilliana watched as he climbed the stairs to his room. "Always at this time of year," she added, almost to herself.

"Why?"

"Something that happened a long time ago."

"What was it?"

"A first love. Sometimes the heaviest love of all."

"Why is it the heaviest?"

"A first love leaves a deep imprint that you carry forever."

"Who was it?"

"You know, I wouldn't recognize you if you ever stopped asking questions." Lilliana pulled the curtain closed. "Someone very special."

"Is that the only reason he's sad?"

"Mostly." Lilliana sank back into her bed, holding

up the quilts for Aurelie to slide in alongside her. "And, apart from that, it's not my business to tell. Now, how about that story you came to read me?"

Aurelie frowned, knowing that once Lilliana ended a conversation, it was closed. She reached for a book on the bedside table. It was made of handmade paper flecked with lavender flowers and touches of real gold. The pages of Lilliana's diaries were the color of tea, and each word was carefully written in black ink.

"Can I ask one more thing?"

"Just one."

"Did she die, Rolo's love?"

"No, she didn't die, but something broke that Rolo found too hard to fix."

"But—"

"Only one question, remember?" Lilliana lay back with a sigh and Aurelie began reading.

"Has he gone?"

"I think so."

"Did he see us?"

"He would have come looking for us if he had."

Julius and his rat friend, Feagle, lay facedown on the ground behind the merry-go-round.

"Do you think it's a sign we should go?" Feagle asked.

"A sign from who?"

"From above . . . or somewhere where signs come from."

"I think it's a sign you shouldn't have worn that extra-long coat you tripped over that made you drop the cage."

"You told me to wear black . . . My dad's coat was all I had."

Julius lifted his head and crawled out to get a better view of the pier. He pulled his beanie down low. "Let's just get this done."

Feagle crouched beside a large, rat-filled cage. The furry rodents swarmed over one another, struggling for room, tails squirming.

"Come on, little darlings. You're about to go on an adventure." Feagle opened the latch on the cage. The rats stumbled out, falling over one another's fluffy, wriggling bodies, tumbling in their rush to escape.

"There's something special about watching a rat find freedom," Feagle said. "They really are beautiful creatures. Did you know rats are actually very clean and spend hours every day—"

"What are they doing now?" Julius asked.

Feagle squinted through the darkness. "I'm not sure."

The rats began to slow down. They stopped and sniffed the air.

"They're coming back this way," Julius whispered.

Julius and Feagle threw themselves on the ground for a second time, covering their heads with their arms. The rats scrambled over them in panic, their claws digging into their coats and hands, clambering through their hair and down the lengths of their bodies.

"What's happening?" Julius whimpered.

"I dunno. I've never seen 'em act like this before. Maybe it's that sign I spoke about." Feagle gasped. "Or . . . it . . . could be *that*," he stammered.

As the rats retreated in a swarm, Feagle and Julius stared at what seemed to be an almost transparent figure floating above the ground only feet before them. He wore boots, a floppy black hat, and a long beard; a sword hung from his waist below a rumpled shirt. He seemed to be frowning at them.

"What is it?" Julius rubbed his suddenly cold body.

"I'm not sure, but I'm not sticking around to find out." Feagle tucked his cage under his arm and the two young men scurried after the rats, all of which had made a hasty exit from the pier.

Some Bad News

Mayor Bog leaped out of bed the next morning. He felt like a richer man. Richer in the way he had earned a lot of money while simply enjoying a good night's sleep—and no one had been hurt in the process. There might be a few tears, but that was merely part of being human. No one had ever died from crying too many tears.

He'd wait a day before calling the health inspectors to close the pier. The rats would then have time to make their way into cupboards and mattress stuffing, and leave enough trails of droppings to give any health inspector a heart-stopping conniption.

By the end of the week, the problem with the pier should have disappeared. And so would Crook.

Happiness was such an unusual mood for Mayor Bog to be in when he was with his wife and son that they were both startled when he arrived in the breakfast room, not only with a smile, but humming as well.

"You look unseasonably happy today," his wife noted.

"And that is because I am happy." He held his arms out. "Why would I have any reason to be *un*happy?" He smiled and flicked a napkin into the air, catching sight of a model ship on the sideboard. "What is that?"

Rufus's spoonful of scrambled egg stopped before his mouth.

"That is a model of the *Mary Rose*. Rufus made it." Mrs. Bog threw her son a smile.

Mayor Bog dipped a buttered piece of toast into his soft-boiled egg, having forgotten his question halfway through Mrs. Bog's answer.

Rufus brought the spoon into his mouth.

"Don't you want to tell him what a fine job he has done?" Mrs. Bog asked.

The front doorbell echoed around them. Bog frowned.

A house servant in a crisp shirt entered the room. "Sir, your assistant, Julius, requests to see you."

"Ah, Julius." Mayor Bog crunched. "Tell him I'll meet him in the study."

He quickly dipped two more strips of toast into his egg, downing them with noisy sips of tea before dramatically wiping a napkin across his lips.

"Good day to you both. I have urgent business to

attend to with Julius." He nodded toward Rufus. "You would do well to follow Julius's example, my boy. Not just playing with toys." He nodded toward the ship. "Why, it isn't even seven-thirty and he is already here to start work. He would make any father proud."

Rufus opened his mouth but closed it again when Mayor Bog headed out of the room.

Bog patted his well-fed stomach and climbed the stairs to his study, where he was met by Julius's sallow face. His clothes were torn and his hands and face were smeared with dirt.

Bog sat behind his desk and continued to grin as he waited to hear the good news. "You didn't come through the front door like that, did you?"

"Sorry, Mayor, I—"

"Never mind. Tell me how last night went."

"You see, Mayor . . ." Julius clenched his fingers so tightly that they were in danger of snapping off.

"Yes?" ·

"It seems we . . . failed."

Mayor Bog's mood fell, along with the tone of his voice. "Failed?"

"The rats." Julius quickly tried to explain. "Top quality they were—Feagle handpicked them himself—but they . . . ran away."

"Ran away?" Mayor Bog concentrated on not jumping across the desk and strangling him.

"There must have been over a hundred rats in that cage but, when we let them loose, they moved only a few feet, then they turned, and ran off the pier in a panic. Ran all over us." Julius shivered. "Some even jumped off the edge and into the ocean, and after the accident with the cage we thought . . ."

"Accident with the cage?" Mayor Bog's voice deepened even further.

"Ah . . . yes . . . a small accident where the cage kind of fell . . ."

Mayor Bog turned away. He eyed the wastebasket in the corner of the room in case his eggy breakfast decided not to stay put. "Did anyone see you?"

"No, I don't think so."

"Don't *think* so?"

"Definitely not, sir. I'm sure of it." Julius rubbed his eyes, which had dark circles lying beneath them like fat slugs. "No one, that is, apart from . . ." Julius leaned forward, his eyes wide with fear. "A ghost."

The mayor blinked once. "A ghost?"

"Yes, sir. Mean and nasty-looking and—"

"There were no ghosts, Julius, just a monumentally simple task bungled."

"Sorry, sir." The young boy twisted his hands together. "What would you like me to do next, sir?"

Many things flashed through Mayor Bog's mind: a

slow boat to China, the Trans-Siberian Railway, a sled dragged by huskies into the arctic wilderness.

"Nothing. I need time to think. Meet me in the office." When Julius stood, Mayor Bog noticed his fully crumpled state—his untucked shirt, stained trousers and shoes. And there was a smell. "After you have had a shower."

Julius nodded like a battery-operated toy running low on power.

"And use the back exit."

"Yes, sir." He tiptoed quietly out of the room.

Mayor Bog caught sight of himself in the polished silver of his mother's urn. Her stern photo stared back at him with her thick frowning eyebrows and high-collared neckpiece that threatened to strangle her.

"You were right, Mother. If you want something done, you need to do it yourself."

He strode out of his study and down the stairs. With each step his anger sizzled. He snatched his coat from the stand in the foyer and rammed his arms through each of the silk-lined sleeves. He pulled his hat onto his head with a vigor that would keep it fastened in the strongest wind. He swept his umbrella from the stand and opened the door.

"Are you leaving, Mr. Bog?" His wife's voice floated after him. "Because a goodbye would be nice if that was the case."

Mayor Bog gripped the handle of the door and sighed through gritted teeth. He straightened up, turned, and entered the breakfast room, his face filled with a forced smile. "Goodbye to you both."

He turned sharply, his umbrella swinging behind him in a wide enough circle to make contact with the *Mary Rose*. Rufus heard the crack on the hull. The ship swayed briefly on its stand before keeling over onto the marble floor and splintering with a high-pitched crash.

Rufus's hands were clenched so tightly that his nails dug into his palms.

"Oh, Mr. Bog." Mrs. Bog stood, her hands resting on Rufus's shoulders.

Mayor Bog stared at the broken mess. "I will buy you another," he said to Rufus. "An even better one."

Rufus said nothing.

"Yes"—Mayor Bog again pulled down on his already tight hat—"a better one." And he left the room, trailing a gloomy, shattered silence behind him.

An Unexpected Gift

Aurelie skidded her boots across the pebbles on the curved driveway of Mayor Bog's house. She came to a stop in a small whorl of dust when she reached the same sleek limousine she had seen bring Rufus to school. She walked the length of the car and followed her reflection in the smudge-free chrome and through the polished windows. A driver with gloved hands and a hat slung across his face sat asleep at the wheel.

The house was equally as grand, with so many windows Aurelie felt as if she was being watched. She climbed the white marble stairs to the veranda and reached for the shiny brass knocker—when the door swung open.

Mayor Bog stopped mid-stride at the sight of a child on his doorstep. He looked around to see if there were any more of them. "Yes?"

"I'm a friend of your son's."

Mayor Bog stared. "My what?"

"Your son. Rufus. Can I come in and see him?"

Mayor Bog's eyes flew to his sleeping driver. "I'm not sure my son is dressed to receive—"

"It won't take long."

Bog ran his eyes over the child with colorful cheeks and curly, every-which-way hair.

"And who shall I say is calling?"

"Aurelie Bonhoffen."

Mayor Bog's puffed chest deflated. "Who?"

"Aurelie Bonhoffen, and I'd like to—"

"Bonhoffen?" The last of Mayor Bog's fake sincerity left him, and he looked like a man about to be very ill. "You're Aurelie Bonhoffen?"

"Yes. I go to school with Rufus." She leaned in and whispered, "I've brought him a present, but don't tell him. It's a surprise."

"A surprise?" Bog repeated absently, before pointing. "He's in there." He stepped past her. "I must go; I have a very important . . ."

The mayor and the rest of his mumbled sentence moved quickly away. He tapped sharply on the driver's window before wrenching open the back door and climbing inside. He waved the driver on with annoyed flicks of his hand, and the car kicked up pebbles as it swerved down the driveway.

Aurelie wiped her boots and stepped into the foyer. The fine carpets absorbed the sound of her footsteps until she stood at a doorway and looked inside. Rufus was sitting at a long table, staring at the broken hull of the *Mary Rose*.

"What happened?" she asked.

Rufus flinched. "Nothing. It was an accident. My dad's going to buy me a new one. What are you doing here?"

Aurelie stepped closer to the ship with its broken masts and twisted sails.

"But you must have worked so hard to build her."

"It doesn't matter." Rufus pushed the boat aside. "How did you get in here?"

"Your dad let me in." Aurelie reached into her bag and pulled out an object wrapped in fabric. "I wanted to give you this."

Rufus eyed her suspiciously. "Why?"

"You like boats, so I thought you'd like this."

"What is it?"

"If you open it you'll see." Aurelie held the gift out further. "It's not going to explode."

Rufus looked over his shoulder. "I have to—"

"Get to school. Me too. We can walk together."

Rufus took the parcel and picked open the fabric. Inside was a polished brass compass, its magnetic needle flickering across its ivory surface. It smelled old, with a faint hint of the sea and, instead of feeling cold, it warmed his hands.

"Uncle Rolo says it's very old and would have saved a lot of sailors' lives." Rufus said nothing. "And Christopher Columbus said that the compass always seeks the truth. I like that."

"Why are you giving it to me?"

"I told you, you like boats." Aurelie paused. "And I wanted to ask you a favor."

"What kind of favor?" Rufus frowned.

"The pier's in trouble, and I need your help to save it."

"Sniggard was right—you were only being nice because I'm the mayor's son."

"I was being nice because I liked your speech about the *Mary Rose*. I'm asking you to help me because you're good with words."

"Why should I help you?"

"Because you owe me for treating me badly when your friends are around, and because that's a nice compass."

"What do you want me to do?"

Aurelie pulled out a chair and sat facing him. Rufus backed away a little. "I want to ask everyone in Gribblesea who loves the pier to volunteer to rebuild it so it can go back to being as great as it used to be. Then everyone who helps will be invited to a special performance in the big top, just for them, with a brand-new show that has never been seen before."

"What kind of show?"

"I don't know—I've only just thought that bit up—but it'll be great."

"It'll have to be something special," Rufus said. "Does anyone else know about your plan?"

"Not yet. I wanted to tell you first so you could help me write an invitation that nobody can refuse. Will you do it?"

"I'll see."

"Great."

"I didn't say I'd do it."

"You didn't say you wouldn't."

"You like getting your way, don't you?"

"Maybe." She tried to smother a smile. "A little."

"Maybe?" Rufus grinned.

"Yes." Aurelie stood. "I'll tell you the rest of my ideas on the way to school."

His smile fell away. "I . . . I haven't packed my bag yet. You go without me."

"Okay." Aurelie pushed her chair in. "Can I ask you something?"

"Yes?"

"Why do you hang around Sniggard and Charles?"

"They're my friends."

"No, they're not. They bully you into doing things you don't want to do."

"They don't bully me."

"And I'll bet they don't know anything about you."

"They know lots of things about me."

"Do they know what you like to eat or what your favorite book is or what you want to do when you're older?"

Rufus squirmed. "Boys don't talk about that kind of stuff."

"I like waffles with ice cream and hot fudge sauce. I love reading all kinds of books, but my favorite at the moment is about the explorer Marco Polo. And I want to run a pier when I'm older, which is lucky because I live on one now and we're about to fix it up so I can make sure that happens."

"I have to get ready for school," Rufus said.

Aurelie's smile dissolved. "I'll see you there."

Rufus watched through the window as she walked down the driveway. Her red swirling skirt stood out against the gray pebbles, deep green lawn, and perfectly shaped hedges. As she reached the gates, he ran to the front door and yelled from the veranda: "A pilot."

Aurelie looked back. "What?"

"I want to be a pilot when I'm older."

"That's a good choice." She waved.

Rufus waved back and watched her walk out the front gates, the brass compass firmly nestled in his hand.

Uncle Rindolf and Uncle Rolo

There you are." Aurelie threw her hands into the air upon spotting Rolo sitting at the far end of the pier. He was behind the circus tent, in an area closed off to the public and a favorite place for him to think. His legs dangled over the side and his arms threaded through the wooden railing. He was singing. Aurelie smiled at the faint strains of the tune and followed his gaze that led again to the house on the hill, but when she looked back, she stopped. Her breath squeezed from her chest. She blinked and shielded her eyes, thinking the glare of the late-afternoon sun was playing tricks on her.

Rolo seemed to be disappearing.

"Uncle Rolo?" she yelled.

He startled and attempted to stand but bumped

into the railing. He sat down and rubbed his head. "Aurelie. I didn't see you . . . um . . ."

She said nothing.

Rolo held out his hand. "Come here."

Aurelie's heart sent pounding thuds through her body. She slowly walked over to her uncle and sat beside him. She stared at his legs, his shoes, his hands squeezed together in his lap, all now fully visible.

Waves slammed against the support poles beneath them.

"Sea looks a bit edgy. Might be a storm later." Rolo fidgeted, swinging his legs and blowing hair out of his eyes. He tried to catch Aurelie's downcast gaze. "How was school?"

"Good." Aurelie's answer disappeared on the wind as quickly as it was spoken.

"You're lucky. A real natural at learning. I remember when I started to teach you to—"

"You came back, didn't you?"

"What do you mean?" Rolo's nervous laugh flickered between them.

"The Bonhoffen secret. You're the one who came back. And it's got something to do with the house on the hill, hasn't it?"

"Who's been talking to you? Was it Rindolf? He's got such a big mouth. Wait until I—"

"So it's true."

"No, I didn't mean . . . it's just that . . ." Rolo sighed and dropped his head forward. "Yes. It's true."

"So you're a ghost?" She whispered shakily.

"No. Not exactly. I'm still me, too. The same Rolo you've known all your life." He reached his hand out to touch her, but she pulled away.

"I saw you disappearing."

Rolo winced. "It happens sometimes when I'm tired or not concentrating."

Aurelie turned to him. "Like in Mrs. Farnhumple's office? When you fell off the chair?"

Rolo shrugged. "She was going on so much and not making any sense that I . . . switched off."

"That's why you could rescue Rindolf, on the roof, on the night of my birthday?"

Rolo shook his head. "Clumsy fool."

Aurelie sneaked a sideways look. "Are you *real*?"

"Yes, I'm real. I age and ache as I get older. If I hit my head, it hurts. I get hungry and thirsty, just like everybody else. But I also have this kind of extra dimension that other people don't have. Like the disappearing thing you saw . . . or didn't see."

Aurelie eyed him warily. "Lilliana says people who come back can walk through walls."

"It's true, but I don't do that very much. It was

111

exciting at first, but after a while I preferred opening doors in the regular way. Rindo, though, he can get lazy and—"

Aurelie gasped. "Rindolf too?"

Rolo bit down on his lips and slumped. "Yes."

"What happened?"

Rolo paused. "There was an accident. At night. On the western cliff road. Rindolf was driving. It was raining hard, and when the road twisted at Deadman's Bend, a rabbit jumped in front of the car. Rindolf swerved to avoid it, but the wheels lost their grip and we went over the edge."

"And you died," Aurelie said softly.

"For a few seconds. Until we decided to come back."

Aurelie's gaze dropped into the swirling ocean. "So you're not like a regular uncle?"

"Oh." Rolo took a hanky from his jacket and blotted Aurelie's cheek. "I am every inch your uncle. I'm not sure you can call me regular in too many ways." He sat straighter. "But if being a 'regular uncle' means that I'd jump from the tallest building or throw myself in front of a pack of wild horses to save you, then, yes, regular is what you'd call me."

"You didn't get the scar from a knife-throwing trick, did you? And your leg—you don't limp because you fell from a horse."

Rolo shook his head. "When the car toppled over

the cliff, I cut my forehead on the windshield, and the steering wheel jammed into my leg. Other than that, I am alive, exactly the same as I was before the crash. Except for a few ghostly qualities."

"When did it happen?"

"Before you were born."

"Does Lilliana know?"

"They all know." Rolo bent his head and tried to meet her eyes.

"What did it feel like"—she winced—"when you died?"

"Like being under water. Everything was slow and muffled. We were trapped in Rindolf's car at the bottom of the cliff, perched on a boulder, tilting this way and that, threatening any minute to be pulled into the sea. But we weren't afraid because, well . . . we'd both died the moment the car hit the rocks." Aurelie felt her breath squeezed out of her chest. "But we came back."

"For the woman in the house on the hill?"

Her uncle nodded. "Please don't be scared, I . . ." He reached out to touch her.

"I have to go." Aurelie grabbed the railing and pulled herself up. Rolo watched her run away and only just miss colliding with a dark figure before disappearing into the night.

The silhouette walked toward Rolo and sat beside him. "She knows?" Rindolf asked.

"She knows." A single tear fell down Rolo's cheek.

"She'll be okay. She just needs time."

Rindolf put his arm around his brother's shoulder, and the two of them stayed on the pier for what felt like hours.

A Brilliant Plan

Mayor Bog hadn't slept all night. The weight of his weariness sank into his body and he slouched over onto his desk. Only his hand moved, slowly circling one word with a pen: Bonhoffen.

"Bonhoffen. Bonhoffen." He circled and scribbled until he had obliterated the name with ink.

His hair was wild and his eyes were red and blood-shot.

The phone sprang to life at his elbow. Bog stared in horror before gathering his breath and doing his best to sound calm. "Hello?"

"Bog? It's Crook. When can I have my pier?"

"Mr. Crook," Bog oozed. "What timing—I was working on the final details now."

"So it will happen by the end of the month?"

"Just as you asked." Bog wiped his brow with his sleeve. "And might I say how grateful the town will—"

Bog's ear rang with the click of Crook hanging up. He replaced the receiver and dropped his pen onto the desk. It rolled across a newspaper and stopped, pointing to a headline:

DELINQUENCY ON OUR STREETS

by Percy Codswothel

Gribblesea citizens have been at the mercy of a spate of child delinquency. Police have been faced with an increase in the number of broken shop windows, snatched purses, and stolen garden gnomes. This outburst of wayward behavior . . .

Mayor Bog's reading was interrupted by a knock at the door.

"What?" he shouted.

A member of his house staff entered and bowed. "Mrs. Bog asked me to let you know breakfast is ready, sir."

"Yes. Right. Coming."

He hoisted his body upright, ran a hand carelessly across his hair, and caught a brief look at his tousled and unshaven reflection in the mirror before sighing and turning away.

"Dear me, Mr. Bog." Mrs. Bog stared at his wild hair, crooked robe, and slippered feet. "Is something wrong?"

Mayor Bog felt like telling his wife that everything

116

was wrong. That his career and reputation were on the brink of ruin, and they were about to lose the life that had taken years to build.

But all he said was, "Sorry, dear. Bad sleep."

"Bad sleep or not, we must still maintain standards."

"Yes, dear," he mumbled. "Standards."

The clatter of knives, forks, and teacups was the only noise to fill the room before Mrs. Bog spoke up. "Rufus and I have been having a lovely chat. Is there anything you'd like to ask him?"

Both Mayor Bog and Rufus looked up.

"Ask him?"

"Yes," Mrs. Bog answered.

Mayor Bog lifted his fork. "How are you, son?"

"Good." Rufus coughed and almost choked on his toast.

"He's good," Bog reported to his wife.

"And perhaps you'd like to ask him how school is?"

"School?" Mayor Bog stopped in the middle of dipping another piece of toast into his runny yellow egg.

"Yes," Mrs. Bog said. "School."

Mayor Bog sighed. "How . . . is school?"

"Fine, sir."

Mayor Bog smiled overly wide. "You see, dear? School's fine."

Mayor Bog and Rufus turned back to their breakfasts.

"You could ask after his friends," Mrs. Bog said.

117

Mayor Bog looked up with a strained smile. "And how," he asked, "are your friends?"

"Good."

"And there you are, my dear; his friends are—"

"I have a new friend," Rufus found himself saying. "She's funny and knows how to juggle and reads books on explorers and her name's Aurelie Bonhoffen. She was named after her great-great-grandmother and it means golden, only she was in trouble with the principal the other day, who thinks she's a delinquent, but she isn't because—"

"Did you say *Bonhoffen*?" Mayor Bog eyed his son with renewed interest.

"Yes." Rufus noticed an unusual glint in his father's eye. "Aurelie Bonhoffen."

"And she's a *delinquent*?"

"She's different from other kids, but I don't think so. In fact, she gave me—"

"I read an article recently about delinquency," Bog mused.

"But she's not—"

"It said delinquency was the fault of the parents." Bog stood abruptly, dropping his spoon with an eggy splat. "My boy." He kissed Rufus on the head. "I'm glad we had this chat."

Rufus's smile was unsure as his father hurried from the room.

In his study, Mayor Bog laughed, quietly at first, then louder. The full width of his belly wobbled at each chuckle. He strolled over to his mirror. His eyes rose from his slippers to his now victorious face. "You, Mayor Bog, are a genius."

He winked at himself and flicked his unkempt hair out of his eyes.

"And the best thing of all," he said with a syrupy grin, "it's perfectly legal. Not only that, it will be in the best interests of Aurelie Bonhoffen."

"How kind, Mayor Bog, to take time out of your busy schedule to have tea this afternoon."

Mayor Bog was sitting in his council office with a small table of cakes, cups, and teapots between him and the principal of Gribblesea Academy.

"I don't mean to sound my own trumpet, Mrs. Farnhumple, but I think it is the mark of a good mayor when he or she takes an interest in the education and well-being of the town's school children. Oh, and this is for you." Bog opened a desk drawer and pulled out a small, but very expensive, box of chocolates.

"Why thank you, Mayor Bog. You are really too kind. And, might I say, the statue being built in your honor is not a moment too soon in coming."

"Yes, well, one doesn't have time to think about statues when there's a town to look after. Take, for example, the current spate of juvenile delinquency and numerous concerns from the public about the pier."

"Concerns?"

"Yes, there have been suggestions of rats, chaos, and somewhat loose moral behavior. I worry for the children who frequent the pier, but particularly the Bonhoffen girl who lives there."

Mrs. Farnhumple's eyes widened at the mention of Aurelie, and she held her chocolate éclair aloft. "I've had my concerns about that girl for some time."

"Have you?" asked Mayor Bog.

"Yes, I've always thought the pier was no place for a child to live. It stays open past dark and is full of characters not fit for a young girl to mix with. On some occasions, when I've been passing, I've seen teenagers out well after the hour they should be home. When I spoke to the girl's uncles recently about correct behavior for students, they seemed to have no idea what I was talking about."

"It does sound serious." Mayor Bog nodded, using one of his most concerned looks. "What do you suggest we do?"

"I think it would be a good time for Saint Barnabas to investigate, before we lose what should be a fine young girl."

Saint Barnabas was a group of concerned Gribblesea citizens. Its full title was Saint Barnabas's Society for the Welfare of Young People and Encouragement of Good Manners, and Mrs. Farnhumple was one of its key members.

"You must do as you see fit," Mayor Bog offered. "My assistant, Julius, will be at your service if you need him."

"You are a good, kind man, Mayor Bog."

The mayor looked away humbly. "Call me Finnigus."

Mrs. Farnhumple blushed. "Of course, Finnigus."

A Ghostly Demonstration

I know what I'm doing, Frank." Rolo turned from the broken generator beside the tent and pointed a wrench into the air. "I've done this a million times."

"It'll be best if you just let him do it, Frank," Rindolf said over his shoulder. "You know how stubborn Old Grumpy can get."

"It's not about being stubborn or grumpy, I—"

"Shhh." Rindolf caught sight of Aurelie weaving through the afternoon crowds of the pier.

"What do we do?" Rolo asked.

"Act normally," Rindolf answered.

"Act normally how?"

"I know acting normally is hard for you," Rindolf said, "but just try."

The two men turned their attention back to the

generator. Rolo began whistling a lively tune when Aurelie walked up behind them.

"Aurelie, sweetheart!" Rolo said with more than a little surprise. "Look, Rindolf, it's Aurelie. We were just acting normally, fixing the generator, and who should walk up behind us but our favorite niece!"

Rindolf threw his rambling brother a frown. "How was school?"

"Good."

"Good."

Aurelie scuffed her shoe into the ground. "I'm sorry I ran away from you before, Rolo."

Rolo scrambled to his feet and clutched the wrench before him. "Oh, but you needed to. You had to. What else could you do?"

"I was scared."

"There's no need to be scared. No need at all. What can I do to make you feel better?"

"You can be more careful about where you are when you disappear," Aurelie scolded. "Make sure no one's around who doesn't know."

"I will." Rolo put his hand on his heart. "I promise. No more disappearing in inappropriate places."

"And I'd like something else," Aurelie said.

"What? Anything. You name it and it's yours."

"I want to know about coming back."

Rindolf and Rolo swapped a careful look.

"What would you like to know?" Rolo asked.

"Lilliana says people who come back have the marks of a ghost. Is that true?"

"Yes," said Rolo. "There's the walking through walls and . . ."

"I'd like to see it."

Rindolf stood beside his brother. "It's a little . . . *unusual* at first. Are you sure you want to see?"

"Yes."

Rindolf held open a flap of the tent. "Then let the show begin."

Rolo threw the switch for the lights. Above the circus ring were two giant, painted angels suspended between strings of colored lights.

Aurelie sat in the front row of the stands.

"If you get frightened, we can stop," Rolo said.

She shook her head. "I won't be frightened."

Rolo and Rindolf took canes, top hats, and suitcases from an old trunk of props and stood at either end of the tent. They began walking toward each other. Rolo tipped his hat to imaginary people before coming across Rindolf. "Ah, good morning, old chap."

Both men put their cases down and shook hands.

"And good morning to *you*. What a glorious day!"

"Ah, I say, old chap . . . it seems you are disappearing."

"Oh bother." Rolo began to fade. "I think you might

be right. Cheerio, then." He continued to disappear until even his gleaming smile was a memory.

Rindolf looked around and sat beside the suitcases. He opened Rolo's, took out an imaginary sandwich, and began to eat. "He won't be needing this then."

Rolo reappeared and knocked Rindolf's hat off his head. "Hey! That's *my* lunch."

Rindolf's cheeks bulged with the imaginary sandwich. "'orry."

The two men stood and bowed.

"What else can you do?" Aurelie asked.

Rolo stole behind a side curtain and into the wings while Rindolf grabbed a newspaper from the trunk and stuck it under his arm. He whistled as he strolled across the ring toward the giant support pole in the center. As he walked, he looked at his watch and, just as he should have collided with the pole, stepped right through it, stopping on the other side to read his paper.

Rolo drove out in a small pedal car from behind large black curtains. He spun the wheel back and forth as if he'd lost control. He honked the horn twice at Rindolf as the car swerved all over the ring. He honked again, but still Rindolf wouldn't move. The car swerved closer, turning until it drove straight through him. Rindolf turned the page of his paper and continued reading.

Rolo wiped his brow in exaggerated relief, until the

car swung around toward Rindolf again. But, just as the car was about to slide through him, Rindolf rose from the floor as if he was being pulled upward by invisible strings. The car drove under him and straight into the pole. Steam shot out of the engine as Rindolf floated back to earth and rushed to help a dizzy Rolo from the car.

The two uncles held their hands in the air and bowed.

"How does it work?" Aurelie asked quietly. "When I touch you, you feel real."

"It's like we can decide to be fully human or mostly human with ghostly bits thrown in," Rolo explained. "It's all a matter of concentration."

"Something Old Forgetful here isn't very good at." Rindolf raised an eyebrow.

"I'll get better," Rolo said to Aurelie. "I promise."

"Can you do anything else?" she asked.

The two uncles raced to the box, pulled out swords, and wrapped shiny capes around their shoulders. They held the swords high as they squared each other off.

Rolo assumed a French accent. "You 'ave inzulted me, my family, ze king, and my horze."

"You are wrong, monsieur," Rindolf replied. "I would never insult anyone's horse!"

"En garde!" Rolo cried, and the two began to fight. Swords clashed and rang throughout the tent. The uncles dodged and thrust until they plunged their swords into each other's bodies.

"Ah! You got me," Rolo cried, and stumbled.

"Ah! You got me too." Rindolf staggered and they both fell to the ground.

They lay with swords protruding from their stomachs until Rolo lifted his head. "You're supposed to clap now."

Aurelie, who had been holding her breath, clapped.

The two men jumped up, withdrew the bloodless swords, and bowed before climbing onto the bench on either side of their niece.

"We're sorry we didn't tell you earlier," Rolo said. "We always meant to, but it was hard to work out when."

"Is there anything else I should know?" Aurelie asked.

"Should we tell her about Frank?" Rindolf asked.

Rolo's face soured. "He'll only show off like he always does."

"Who's Frank?"

Rindolf called. "Come on out, Frank. It's time to say hello."

Aurelie squinted into the streams of dusty light in the tent. Slowly, the shabby form of a man appeared. He wore tall black boots, a sword at his side, a rumpled shirt, and a floppy black hat perched on wild curly hair.

"Aren't you going to introduce me?"

Rolo crossed his arms. "Aurelie, this is Frank. Frank, this is Aurelie. Happy?"

"Never mind him, dear. He never had many manners before he died, so it's no surprise he has none now that he's come back."

He held out his hand.

Aurelie went to shake, but her hand reached through Frank's. She gasped and withdrew her arm, hugging it to her chest.

"Don't go giving her your hand," Rolo growled. "You don't have one, remember? Or a brain, come to think of it."

"So you're a real ghost?" Aurelie asked.

"Yep." Frank held his hat across his chest. "Died during the storm of 1913. It swept up fast, with winds so fierce that the pier's swinging chair ride was in danger of being uprooted and flung into the ocean. The lives of small children were at risk, and I had to act. Just as I'd pulled all the kids to safety, one of the chairs snapped free, falling on me, and killing me in an instant."

"Okay, Mr. Hero," Rolo said. "Now tell her how you *really* kicked the bucket."

Frank's shoulders slumped. "Pumpkins."

"Pumpkins?" Aurelie asked.

"Yeah." Frank shrugged. "I was walking through the Alleys when the back of a cart carrying a load of pumpkins broke. They spilled out, and with just one bad bounce on the head I was a goner. I had hoped for a more glorious death."

"Frank sometimes joins us in the ghost train," Rindolf explained.

"I mostly like being the beheaded man on the guillotine." Frank smiled broadly.

"But the beheaded man is a dummy," Aurelie said.

"Most nights it's me. It's more lifelike that way. I never tire of seeing the faces of passengers when my chopped-off head thuds into the wastebasket, my wide, horror-struck eyes staring straight at them. I've had over fifty pass-outs so far."

"Pass-outs?"

"You know, fainters. Like this." Frank collapsed to the floor dramatically.

Rolo frowned. "Did I mention he was a show-off?"

"Are you the only ghost who works here?"

Frank opened his eyes and shot a look at Rindolf. "How much have you told her?"

"We've just started, really."

Frank jumped up and rubbed his ghostly hands together. "Come on out, fellas!"

A straggly group of men and women wavered into view. Jugglers, ride operators, circus masters, horse riders. Some waved, others bowed or curtsied.

Aurelie's face paled. "You're all ghosts?"

"It's okay, sweetie." Rindolf hugged her close. "We've known them for years."

"Some longer than others," answered the circus master who had fluffy eyebrows and a beard like a small cloud. He bowed and tipped his tall hat. "I'm Master Dudley Dragoon—first circus master of Gribblesea Pier."

"So that means you were born . . ." Aurelie began.

"One hundred and thirty years ago. But I do think I hold my age rather well, don't you?"

"Yes." Aurelie smiled. "You look quite handsome."

Master Dudley blushed.

Aurelie crossed her arms and rubbed her shoulders. "Is anyone else suddenly cold?"

Rolo took off his jacket and wrapped it around her.

"Sorry." Frank screwed up his face. "That's our fault, I'm afraid. Ghosts have a habit of sending the temperature down."

"How come I've never seen any of you?"

"We have to want you to see us," explained a tall man with a riding crop and short red jacket. "And we wanted you to be okay with it first."

"Most of them used to work here years ago," Rindolf said. "It's only Frank who still likes to help out."

"It takes time to get used to," Rolo added. "We're still here for you, though, like we've always been."

"Always will be." Rindolf smiled.

"Us too"—a round woman in a flouncy red dress

winked—"now that we've finally met. I'm Rosie." She turned and introduced the others. "And that's Hamish, Glenda, and Roberto."

The three ghosts waved.

A tear balanced on the tip of Aurelie's eyelash. The uncles opened their arms and wrapped her in their capes.

"Is it too much, all at once?" Rolo held her hands. "I knew it'd be too much."

"No, it's just . . ." Aurelie took a breath. "You're not going anywhere, are you?"

"Nowhere that doesn't involve being near you," Rolo said. "What would be the point of that?"

"No point at all." Rindolf shook his head.

Master Dudley wiped his sleeve across his eye and motioned for the others to leave. They took a few steps before disappearing.

"Is there anything else you'd like to know?" Rolo asked.

"Why did you decide to come back?"

Rolo was quiet.

"We needed to see someone," Rindolf answered.

"The woman in the house on the hill?"

"Valentina Bloomfield," Rolo said quietly. "She was beautiful. She reminded me of music, the way she talked and laughed."

"What happened?"

"I was on my way to ask her an important question when we had the accident. That's why I came back."

"And I came back 'cause I'd watched these two love-birds for months—I had to make sure his nerves wouldn't stop him from going through with it."

"But when we got to the house, it was too late," Rolo said. "Through the window we saw the son of one of the town's richest families. His name was Reinfeld. He was on one knee holding out a ring." Rolo laughed. "I couldn't compete with him. He was rich and handsome with a big house, and I was a circus man with a trumpet, some juggling skills, and not much else."

"A month later," Rindolf continued, "we read in the paper that Reinfeld was getting married, but not to Valentina. I rushed to tell Rolo, just as he got her letter."

"It said she was leaving Gribblesea to set up a charity for homeless children in the city," Rolo explained.

"What else did she say?" Aurelie asked.

"She hoped I was well."

"No, when you told her how you felt?"

"I . . . she . . . you see . . ."

Aurelie's eyebrows shot up. "You didn't tell her."

"By the time we got to the house she was already gone. We asked her sister to let her know we'd called, but Valentina never contacted us."

"We tried a few times to find her, but we never could," Rindolf said.

Rolo stubbed his toe into the ground. "I figured she'd forgotten about me by then."

Aurelie threw up her hands. "How could she? You're Rolo—she'd never have forgotten you."

"She probably lives far away in a palace or a fancy London mansion."

"We could try to find her together."

Rolo looked at his watch. "Oh, look at that. We need to get you some dinner before it's time for the evening trains."

"But—" Aurelie objected.

"No 'buts.'" Rolo took her hand and led her to the exit. "Those passengers aren't going to scare themselves, you know."

Frank slumped on the props trunk and watched them leave. "Oh yeah, don't worry about me," he called after them. "I'm just a ghost. No point saying goodbye."

Aurelie stopped. "Bye, Frank."

Frank wore a delighted grin. "It was nice to finally meet you. I'll come and see you when you need a break from those two."

Outside the tent, Rindolf hurried alongside his brother. "Aurelie has a point, you know. Maybe it's time you—"

"Got ready for work?" Rolo interrupted. "I couldn't agree more!"

"No, Rolo." Aurelie puffed beside his quickening steps. "Time you—"

"Look." Rolo pointed into the distance. "Isn't that your friend?"

Rufus ducked under the helium balloons of a young girl and made his way to a smiling Aurelie.

"I accept," she said.

"I haven't said anything."

"You've come to help save the pier, haven't you?"

"Well, yes."

"Save the pier?" Rolo shook his hand. "I knew you looked like a good man the moment I saw you."

"What's the plan?" Rindolf asked.

"We're going to ask for the town's help to rejuvenate the pier in return for a special performance."

"What kind of performance?" Rolo asked.

"It has to be something remarkable," Rufus said. "Something so spectacular that the audience will think they've seen magic."

"Magic." Aurelie turned to her uncles. "That's exactly what we need. Think you can do it?"

"Think so?" Rindolf gave Aurelie a wink. "With the help of a few friends, I think we can give them a performance that will make them think they've seen *ghosts*."

A Surprise Visit

It didn't take long for Mrs. Farnhumple to enlist the help of Ernestine Bloomfield. A fellow member of Saint Barnabas, Ernestine was a rich, miserly woman who, it was rumored, had sewn all the family's wealth into every cushion, mattress, and curtain hem of her mansion overlooking Gribblesea.

"I almost lost my sister to a no-good time-waster of a man from this place." Ernestine adjusted her gloves with a sharp tug and looked up as they approached the pier. "He had her swooning over his fancy words and wily ways, and even led her to believe he intended to marry her."

"What happened?" Mrs. Farnhumple asked.

"He broke her heart, as I warned her he would. Said he would be at our house on a certain evening to ask for her hand, and he never showed up. I promised, from that moment on, I would never let anyone hurt her again. We are sisters, after all, and need to look after each other until the end."

"Well said," Mrs. Farnhumple agreed. "For if you do not have family, who indeed do you have?"

Their conversation halted as they arrived at the gates.

"It's even more run-down than I thought," Ernestine said.

"I suspect inside will be more of the same."

"Wouldn't it be better to visit while Aurelie is here?" Julius panted, having caught up with the two women and their fast-paced steps. He clutched a leather briefcase in one hand and a folder of papers in the other. "To get a proper idea of how she lives? From the girl, I mean."

Mrs. Farnhumple narrowed an eye at the young man. "No need for the little dear to be home for our visit. It would only add to her already unfortunate circumstances."

"Oh, I see, but wouldn't it—" Julius's folder slipped from his hand, sending papers scuttling onto the ground.

Mrs. Farnhumple's eyebrows darted up her forehead. She spun on her heels and led the way through the pier, not pausing for an instant until she stood before the office of Argus Bonhoffen.

Her knock was met with Argus's unshaven face and wild morning hair.

"Mr. Bonhoffen? I'm Mrs. Farnhumple, principal of

Gribblesea Academy, and this is Ernestine Bloomfield, and our assistant, Julius."

"Well hello, ladies, always a pleasant surprise to be met with beauty in the morning. And you too, Julius. This is my wife, Amarella."

"Would you like to come in for tea?" Wisps of hair curled around Amarella's face.

"I'm afraid we don't have time for tea, Mrs. Bonhoffen. We're here as members of the board of Saint Barnabas." Mrs. Farnhumple said this as if to explain everything.

Argus and Amarella stared back.

"We see to the welfare of young people," Ernestine explained.

"Oh, good," Argus said. "The welfare of young people is definitely worth seeing to."

"As you know," Mrs. Farnhumple continued, "we have been having a few problems with Aurelie's behavior at school and—"

"Aurelie's in trouble at school?" Amarella asked.

"I'd assumed your daughter told you. Her uncles came to speak to me only days ago."

"They did?" Amarella looked to Argus, who shrugged.

"Yes, and I must say your not knowing only adds to my concern."

"What kind of trouble has she been in?" Argus asked.

"Well, recently she threw a paint bomb at a teacher."

Amarella looked at her husband then back to the two women. "Are you sure you're talking about *our* Aurelie?"

"Oh yes, Mrs. Bonhoffen. I am."

"What can we do?" Amarella asked uneasily.

"We're here today to ask ourselves that exact question. We believe that by seeing Aurelie's home, we may come closer to the answer."

"If you think it will help," Argus offered. "Where would you like to start?"

"Perhaps a general look at where Aurelie spends her time." Mrs. Farnhumple took a notebook from a handbag.

Argus looked around him. "Let's start with the big top then. Aurelie is becoming quite the performer and is a fast learner."

Argus slipped his hand into Amarella's and led the small group to the tent. He held open the canvas entrance, and the two women hoisted their dresses up over the dusty ground. Julius tripped on an iron tent peg and careered through the flap, falling face-first into an open props box.

"A little more care, Julius." Mrs. Farnhumple stepped over him. "We don't want to lose you before this is over."

Julius struggled upright and brushed himself down.

He smiled at the sight of the tiered seats, painted angels, and walls of bright blue clouds.

"Aurelie loves helping out with the shows," Amarella explained. "Our animal show is a real treat with the kids. No live animals, of course, just performers in costumes. Mostly Aurelie helps out by being the back end of a cow."

"Yes." Ernestine pursed her lips. "We've heard."

"She also helps out with the ghost train." Argus smiled. "She's always been like that. Wanting to help where she can."

"And what does she *do* in the ghost train?" Ernestine asked.

"Sometimes she's the murdered maiden, other times she plays the headless schoolgirl." Argus laughed. "You should see the reaction she gets. Whole carriages screaming in terror."

Ernestine's face drained of color.

Mrs. Farnhumple took hurried notes. "Can we see where the child sleeps?"

"Sure, this way." Argus motioned toward the exit.

"I know a parent is bound to say this," he said, following them outside. "But Aurelie hasn't been an ounce of trouble since she was born."

"Mmm." Mrs. Farnhumple stepped over the congealed puddle of an upturned ice cream.

They walked on in silence.

"Here we are." Argus held his hand out to the ghost train entrance.

"'Here we are' where?" Ernestine's eyes lowered into an irritated squint as they stood before skeletons holding scythes, wild-haired witches on brooms, and carriages fashioned into ghoulish, winged demons.

"Aurelie's bedroom. Well, not *here* exactly."

Argus climbed the front steps to the entrance of the train, which was guarded by a bent, wart-covered troll with a crooked smile and broken teeth. He patted the troll absentmindedly on the head before leading them to a set of narrow stairs at the side. "She sleeps up there."

"Up there?" Mrs. Farnhumple looked as if someone had asked her to hold a python.

"Yep. Please, go on up."

The two women climbed the stairs and disappeared through Aurelie's door.

"What are they looking for?" Amarella whispered to Argus.

"I'm not sure."

It only took minutes for the two women to reappear.

"The best room in the house," Argus said. "With a view of the ocean that would fill even the meanest person with wonder."

Ernestine sucked in a sharp breath, her lips pursed. "I'm going to have to disagree with you, Mr. Bonhoffen.

It is drafty, small, and has none of the things a young girl her age should have—dolls, a set of hairbrushes. The curtains are patchworked rags, and she sleeps above the devilish art and general horror of a ghost train."

"Well, I . . . I . . ." Argus looked around, puzzled.

"We have seen enough. Thank you, Mr. and Mrs. Bonhoffen." Mrs. Farnhumple led the small group through the maze of cotton candy stands, gaming booths, and statues of laughing clowns. Julius turned back to offer his hand in goodbye but fumbled his briefcase and folder, his papers again falling from his grasp. He scrambled after them.

"Come on, Julius." Mrs. Farnhumple's voice cut through the air. Julius clutched the papers to his chest, nodded at the Bonhoffens, and hurried after the women of Saint Barnabas.

"What did they want, Argus?" Amarella breathed.

"I don't really know. Only you're not to worry. I'm sure we can sort out whatever it is." He smiled and kissed Amarella on the cheek. "Meanwhile, Rindolf and Rolo have some explaining to do about that school visit—and it better be good."

A Sad Farewell

Am I to read from this that you are suggesting the girl be removed from her home?"

Mayor Bog held the hastily written report on Aurelie Bonhoffen, requesting her removal from the pier.

"Not only removed, Mayor Bog, but removed immediately."

"So it is as serious as I thought?"

"Gravely serious, sir."

The mayor ran his stubby fingers over the black ink. "At least we have comfort knowing we are providing the girl with opportunities she'd otherwise never have."

"Indeed," Mrs. Farnhumple said. "My only hope is that we will be in time to undo the damage already done."

"The council and I have an important session after lunch and, owing to the urgency of the situation, I'm sure I can have this approved as quickly as possible."

"You are a good man, Mayor Bog."

Bog stared at the report as if his mind was somewhere else. "Pardon? Yes, well. A good man. Indeed."

"It's brilliant!" Rufus blushed as Aurelie declared for the fifth time that his invitation was brilliant. "Really brilliant."

She stood in her overalls in the circus tent where she and her uncles were painting props for the performance. She held the flyer carefully in her hands and read dramatically: "Bonhoffens' Phantasmagoria."

"It's got a lovely ring to it," Rindolf said.

"It means a series of images that make you feel as if you're in a dream," Rufus explained. "I thought it was the perfect name for the show."

"I've done many performances in my life," Rolo said, "but I've never been involved in a phantasmagoria before."

Aurelie read out the whole flyer:

Welcome to
Bonhoffens' Phantasmagoria!
Gribblesea Pier invites you to partake in a weekend
of repairs and rejuvenation of this town's finest attraction.
In return, you will enjoy a never-before-seen performance
of spectacular proportions that will delight,
amaze, and bedazzle.

"We just have to add the dates," Rufus said.

"I knew you were the one to help." Aurelie threw her arms around Rufus. He blushed even more.

"Not only is he a good man; he's smart too." Rindolf wrapped his arms around both of them.

"Come on, my turn." Rolo wiped his eyes and joined in the hug. "And for your reward, you get to have a sneak preview of . . . the Box of Incredulity!"

"The box of what?" asked Rufus.

"Incredulity. Sit with me and you'll see." Aurelie jumped up into the tiered seats and patted the bench beside her. "Everyone's been preparing so hard for the show. Lilliana's even helping To and Fro with a brand-new trapeze act. She was one of the best, so it's going to be brilliant!"

The big top lights dimmed to black. Slowly, one spotlight spilled down over the tall, skinny, upright box. On the front, in letters framed by a swirling mist, Rolo had painted THE BOX OF INCREDULITY.

The uncles could be seen standing on either side of it. Rindolf held two large cymbals, and Rolo held his hands behind his back.

"Lady Aurelie and Gentleman Rufus," Rolo cried, "welcome to Bonhoffens' Phantasmagoria! A show where you will be mesmerized and astounded, fascinated and flabbergasted. Why, you may even be *mesmeroundedfascingasted*!"

Rindolf clapped the cymbals together.

"I am the Riveting Rolo, and he is the Rambunctious Rindolf." They both bowed. "And this is the Box of Incredulity."

Rindolf clanged the cymbals again, only this time so close to Rolo's ear that his eyes crossed and he teetered from side to side.

"Sorry about that." Rindolf shrugged.

Aurelie and Rufus smiled.

"Why incredulity?" Rolo regained his balance and pulled a giant saw from behind his back. "Because I can saw a person in two through it, right before your very eyes."

Rindolf's eyes shot wide open. "What?"

"Don't worry. It won't hurt a bit." He pointed the saw toward the box. "Please step inside."

Rindolf hesitated. "Are you sure?"

"I haven't lost a man yet."

Rindolf placed the cymbals on the ground and rubbed his palms against his trousers. He edged toward the box.

"That's the way," Rolo encouraged him.

He slipped inside and Rolo closed the door behind him.

"I, the Riveting Rolo, am now going to saw the Rambunctious Rindolf in half."

A muffled scream came from inside the box.

"There is absolutely nothing to worry about," Rolo cried. "Not when we have the Box of Incredulity!"

A small whimper was heard as Rolo lined up his saw against the side of the box and began to move the blade forward and backward, slicing and cutting. Wood shavings sprinkled onto the ground.

"Will he be okay?" Rufus asked.

"Sure he will." Aurelie smiled. "Watch."

The blade reached halfway. Rolo stopped to wipe his brow before recommencing. The blade ate further into the box, its teeth protruding through the other side, until finally it had sawed right through. He dropped the blade and took a deep breath.

"And now, let's see how our good friend Rindolf is."

Rolo flung open the door. Rindolf stood inside, his eyes shut tight. "You can come out now."

Rindolf slowly felt his body: his legs, his stomach, his face.

"See?" Rolo asked. "In the Box of Incredulity, you're perfectly safe."

Rindolf stepped out. The two brothers held their hands in the air and bowed.

"Bravo!" Rufus and Aurelie cried out.

Rindolf stepped toward their seats, but when he did his top half went one way and his legs went the other. His top half bowed.

"Ah . . . Rindolf?" Rolo stared at his sawed-off brother.

"What is it? I'm enjoying . . . aaah!"

Rolo pulled the two halves of his brother together, shoved him into the box, and began to wheel him out of the tent, muffled cries coming from inside.

Aurelie jumped to her feet and applauded.

"But that really looked like Rindolf was in two pieces." Rufus's mouth hung open.

"I know." Aurelie clapped and cheered. "I told you they were good."

It was precisely 7 a.m. the following day when Mrs. Farnhumple, Ernestine Bloomfield, Julius, and two police officers arrived at the pier.

"Wretched wind." Ernestine grabbed at her hat and held it in place. Her skirt, however, was whisked into the air, revealing a generous portion of her leg.

Her shriek coincided with the two police officers smirking and turning away.

"Let's go," she growled.

Ernestine knocked on Argus's office door. She could hear nothing over the constant squawking of seagulls. She knocked again.

"Mr. Bonhoffen? Are you in there?"

A window in the building beside her opened and

Argus, wearing only an undershirt, poked his head out into the morning light.

"Oh, Mr. Bonhoffen!" Ernestine and Mrs. Farnhumple spun away. "We'd, um . . . like to talk to you."

"Certainly." Argus shielded his eyes and shook his head to wake himself up. "I'll be right down."

Argus disappeared from his bedroom window and reappeared at the door, pulling his shirt over his head. "Bit of a late night last night. We're planning a big performance, and we got a little carried away."

"Carried away?" Mrs. Farnhumple stared at the disheveled man in front of her.

"You know how it is with musicians. Once you hand them a mandolin and an accordion, there's no stopping them."

Mrs. Farnhumple and Ernestine Bloomfield had no idea how it was with musicians.

Argus felt their silence like a piano string pressing against his neck. He stepped back. "What can I do for you?"

Mrs. Farnhumple nodded to Julius, who searched through his briefcase, took out an important-looking piece of paper, and began reading: "By order of the . . ."

"What is it, Argus?" Amarella pulled her long woolen jacket tightly around her chest and blinked into the cold sunlight.

"I'm not sure, but I'm about to find out."

"Don't let these people stand there in the cold. Where are your manners, Argus? Please, come in."

None of the small group moved.

Ernestine eyed the mayor's young assistant, who stared at the ground. She elbowed him in the ribs. "Julius? Don't you have something to read?"

"Ahh . . . yes, I"—he looked at his paper—"By . . . by order . . . of the . . . Office for the Welfare of . . . Young People and Children, it has been seen fit that due to habits of . . . moral negligence and an unstable living arrangement that . . ."

Julius looked up and caught Amarella's face. The sadness that circled her wide eyes snatched away his ability to read any further.

"I'm sorry. I . . ."

Ernestine grabbed the paper from his hands.

"By order of the Office for the Welfare of Young People and Children et cetera, et cetera, it has been decided, in accordance with Article 327 of the Child Betterment and Protection Act, that Aurelie Bonhoffen be taken from her place of residence at Gribblesea Pier to be placed in another location far more suited to her needs, until the living arrangements of the girl can be altered sufficiently to convince the Office of the fitness of that abode or, in the failure to do so, until the aforementioned child's eighteenth birthday, from whence it will be the child's decision where she may reside."

Argus and Amarella stood rigid. A cold wind swept off the sea.

"Visiting rights allow you to make contact with the child at the discretion of the court-appointed guardian. Refusal to obey the guardian's directions may result in court proceedings against said refuser and a possible jail sentence."

"Jail sentence? Visiting rights?" Amarella slowly repeated the words.

"Yes." Ernestine Bloomfield's nostrils flared slightly. "And as this case is in particular need of urgent attention, a lot of work must be done. So I have decided that there will be no visiting rights until further notice."

"You can't mean this." Amarella's voice was so light it dissolved into the rain that had been threatening all morning to fall.

"Every word of it." Mrs. Farnhumple held her purse over her head. "Julius? The report?"

"Oh . . . um . . . here's a copy of the report and Article 327." He held them out to Argus.

The two policemen looked down at their hats cradled in their hands, the increasing rain dripping down their faces.

Julius pulled his overfilled briefcase to his chest and offered Amarella and Argus the only thing he could: a small, crooked smile.

"You will need to show the officers where the girl is

so they can collect her and a few belongings immediately," Mrs. Farnhumple said.

"Where will she be taken to?" Amarella pushed a drowned curl from her eyes.

"We will let you know when we feel it is appropriate," Ernestine replied.

"Can they do this, Argus?" Amarella asked.

Argus looked down at the report with its small letters crammed together, blotted by rain. "It seems they can."

Argus and Amarella remained fixed to the pier like ice sculptures, with only a moment before they would melt into the sea.

"Mr. and Mrs. Bonhoffen?" Ernestine spoke pointedly. "So we all don't catch our death?"

Argus and Amarella turned and walked toward Aurelie's room. The two women followed, the officers close behind.

"I will go to the courts and sort this out." Great streams of water now ran off Argus's nose. He reached his arms around Amarella and folded her into a hug. She was shaking. Argus held her even tighter to make it stop, but he knew the shivering wasn't from the cold. No matter how close he held her, it would be a long time before she would stop.

Highgate Mansion

I won't!"

Aurelie stamped her foot onto the polished wooden floors of Highgate Mansion, while Ernestine's patience frayed.

"You will and *now!*"

Aurelie kicked the side of the bucket, sending sprays of soapy water into the charged air.

A second woman stepped in. "Perhaps the child needs time to rest. After all, she has only just arrived and maybe—"

"Rest, Sister? There's no time for *rest*. It is imperative that this child learn the essential lessons of life—hard work, discipline, and manners."

"I've learned those things already from my family." Aurelie glared.

"Did they also teach you to respect your elders?"

"Yes, they did, but I'm not sure I see many here worth respecting."

Ernestine's face burned a deep red. "Maybe you'd like to rethink that sentence in your room." Aurelie remained where she was, staring back, hardened and defiant. *"Now."*

If this was a contest, Ernestine had no intention of losing.

Aurelie stepped forward and kicked over the bucket of water before running, two steps at a time, up the curved staircase.

Ernestine stepped away from the spreading puddle. "This is far worse than I thought."

"I'll see if she's okay." The sister turned to climb the stairs.

"Leave her!" Ernestine's fury was like boiling lava. "She will stay there until she learns some manners. Or until she gets hungry enough to realize her failings and apologize. Whichever comes first."

"But she's—"

"Leave her." Ernestine's words jabbed into the air.

"Why is she here?"

"Mayor Bog was worried for her and alerted me to the conditions she was living in at the pier."

"The pier?" The sister's words snagged in her throat.

"Yes. Terrible place to bring up a child. No order, no

decorum. It's even more wretched than it used to be. You should see where she slept, and everywhere you turn there is an overwhelming stench of barnacles and seaweed. She will be better off with us."

"How long do you plan to keep her here?"

"As long as it takes," Ernestine declared.

"And her family? They must be . . ."

"Until they move from that decrepit pier and decide they want to give the girl a proper upbringing, in a proper house, they will have to do without her."

Ernestine called to her housemaid to clean up Aurelie's mess.

"I must leave. I'm due at the mayor's office to report on what has happened. And to tell him the girl is in much more need of our help than I thought."

She snatched a pair of gloves from the side table, fixed her hair in the foyer mirror, and opened the front door.

"Rain," she complained. "Haven't we had enough for one day?" Ernestine seized an umbrella from the hallstand and left.

The sister waited until Ernestine had driven through the front gates before entering the kitchen. She made a hot chocolate with marshmallows, filled a small plate with macadamia cookies, and climbed the stairs to Aurelie's room. She raised her hand to open the door, but the sound of crying stopped her. She drew a steadying breath and knocked.

"Go away!"

"Please, Aurelie, Ernestine has left. Can I come in?"

"I don't want to talk to you."

"Please?"

Silence.

She carefully turned the doorknob. Aurelie stared out the bay window, clutching her knees to her chest. She seemed so small in this grand room filled with antique wardrobes, plump sofas, and chests of drawers covered with doilies and porcelain dolls.

"I thought you might like something to drink." The woman placed the chocolate and cookies on a small side table and stepped away.

Aurelie said nothing. Her eyes were red and her lashes welded together by tears.

"Your being here may seem strange, but my sister is only doing what she thinks is in your best interests . . ."

"Your sister doesn't know anything about me."

She inched closer but Aurelie moved away, squashing herself up against the windowpane. The room had a direct view onto the pier in the far distance. It was clouded in gray rain and a creeping mist.

"Ernestine says you live on the pier?"

Aurelie pulled her knees tighter.

"I loved going to the pier when I was younger. I knew someone who worked there." She said it almost to herself. "It was a long time ago, before you were even born."

Aurelie didn't move.

"He was someone who . . ." She stopped. "Well"—she straightened her skirt—"if you need anything, please ask. We're not bad people, Aurelie. We're only trying to help."

Aurelie's tears and the raindrops on the window blurred her view.

"Your bathroom is through that door. There are fresh towels and soap and specially scented bath lotion if you like."

Aurelie turned to her for the first time. "I want to go home."

"You will. In time. If you need anything, please ask. My name's Valentina."

Aurelie flinched at the mention of her name and turned back to the window. The door clicked shut behind her.

"Valentina," Aurelie whispered, and wedged her chin into the gap between her folded arms. She stared until the day faded into night and she could see the lights of the seafront through the rolling mist. In the center of it was the pier. From anywhere in town you could see it standing out like a many-colored lighthouse: the Ferris wheel, the merry-go-round, the moon-shaped lights that ran the length of both sides. It had withstood some of the ocean's fiercest storms. Some, Lilliana said, that were worthy of knocking the splinters right out of the wooden poles beneath them—but it had never given in.

She smiled as the pier's sign glowed. It blazed into the night until one string of lights burned out. The sign now read: RIBBLESEA PIER.

Aurelie sprang to her knees, flicked the latch on the window, and forced it open. The rain lashed its way in, spilling onto her face and dress.

She held on to the window frame and threaded one leg outside, hooking the toe of her shoe into a square of trellis attached to the wall. Two Dobermans sprang into view. Aurelie snatched her leg inside as they leaped at her, snarling and barking, their sharp teeth glinting in the light from her room.

Soaked through, she pulled the window closed. She took the star ruby from her pocket and held it tightly in her hand. Huddling against the cold glass, she kept watch, afraid that if she took her eyes off the pier, it might disappear forever.

"Pier Closed"

It has come to this." Argus's body slumped forward in his chair, as if it was too heavy for him to keep upright. His elbows leaned into the crumpled pile of bills, notices, and unopened, official-looking letters. "We must sell the pier."

"Sell the pier?" Rolo felt his ears clog with Argus's news and shook his head. "We can't. It's all we have. And Lilliana won't let you."

Lilliana had fallen ill since Aurelie had been taken. She stayed in her bed, buried beneath layers of blankets, looking smaller and paler than her family had ever seen her.

"I've been to the courts," Argus replied. "They consider Aurelie being raised here as an unfit situation for a young girl, and so our only option is to leave." He hauled in a tired breath. "If this is the only way for Aurelie to be with us, then this is what we are going to do."

Amarella sat quietly beside her husband, her eyes dull and clouded by fear.

"I have spoken to Mr. Crook, whose original offer is no longer available, but he has agreed to take it for a lesser price."

"A lesser price?" Rindolf squinted as if this would help him understand. "But his original offer wouldn't have bought the wood that went into building the pier."

"He doesn't want to run it as a pier," Argus confessed quietly. "He said there was no money in that, so he's decided to tear it down and build a luxury hotel instead."

Amarella's eyes snapped shut.

"Tear it down?" Rindolf whispered to himself. "But the pier has been here for over one hundred years."

The rain shuddered against the roof.

"What money we have left after we pay our debts will be divided among everyone here." Argus lowered his head and said, "Amarella and I are sorry."

Rolo stole a look at Amarella's drawn face and rubbed his hands up and down his dirt-smeared overalls. "This will not do!" His head swung high in challenge, and his heart pounded in his chest. "We will not sit here and take this."

Argus held up his hand listlessly. "They have the law behind them." He held out the pages of the report, its rain-blotched creases blurring some words. Rindolf took it and began to read.

Outside, the wind threw fistfuls of rain against the office walls and windows.

"What could they do if we went back to the courts and demanded Aurelie come home?" Rolo asked.

"They could use it as proof that we are willing to ignore the law." Rindolf stared at the report in his hands. "And give them reason to think we are even more unfit to bring up a child responsibly."

Amarella winced but kept her eyes on the floor.

"I'm going to have to ask you to leave," Argus said quietly. "Crook will be here in the morning with papers to sign, and there is a lot to organize before he arrives."

"But—" Rolo began until his elder brother tugged at his sleeve, placed the report on the desk, and led him outside.

Rindolf buttoned his coat against the rain and headed for the shelter of the waffle stand, sitting heavily in a teacup seat. "We have said enough for now."

"But we haven't even begun to have our say." Rolo flicked his rain-soaked hair from his eyes and paced back and forth. "Courts and governments and societies for good manners have been having all the say. Why, if I had my way, I'd step right up to them and—aah!" He stopped abruptly and held his hand to his heart. "I swear, one of these days, Frank . . ."

"Sorry about that." Frank's floating head was joined by his materializing body.

"You've heard?"

"Most of it." Frank pulled his floppy hat off and held it to his chest. "Sad business. Where is she?"

"We don't know, but we're going to get her back," Rolo declared.

"How?" Frank asked.

"We haven't worked that out yet." Rindolf frowned.

"What was the report Argus had?"

"It's from the courts." Rolo kicked the teacup table. "It says the pier's not a fit place for a young girl to live."

"But that's—"

"Crazy." Rindolf nodded. "We know."

"A judge was able to have Aurelie taken because of an article. A small sentence in a law book." Rindolf shivered against the cold.

"Do you remember the number of the article?" Frank asked.

"Article 327 of the Child Betterment and Protection Act." Rindolf said it like he could never forget.

"I know that one."

"You do?" Rolo asked.

"With the decades of spare time I've had since being dead, I often go to the library and read. Especially at night when it's quiet. I find the law very interesting. In fact, if I hadn't been so good at entertaining crowds, I would have made a crackerjack lawyer."

"Do you know any way around it?" Rolo perked up.

"I'd need to read the court's notes." Frank pulled his hat back on his head.

"We need to have a plan before Argus signs those papers tomorrow morning," Rolo added. "Think you can do it?"

"Not if we stand here talking about it." Frank gave them a toothy grin. "Gentlemen, we've got a courthouse to break into."

A Rescue Plan

Aurelie woke in the night to the sound of barking dogs. Huddled beneath a blanket in the bay window of her room, she quickly rose to her knees and put her hands against the pane in time to see two Dobermans race past.

She blinked and rubbed her eyes as Ernestine rushed onto the lawn. Her hair was piled under a scarf, and a long robe swept around her feet as she swung a flashlight over the grounds. The dogs' barking reached the far end of the property, where it suddenly stopped. Moments later they hurtled back, stumbling over each other and cowering around Ernestine's heels with pitiable whines. She patted one of them on the head and kept her flashlight trained toward the front driveway of the house.

"What is it, boys?" She moved forward and urged the dogs to follow, but they cowered even lower. She shook her head and marched into the night alone. The dogs whimpered and backed away before running in the opposite direction.

Aurelie carefully opened the window and stuck her head outside. The rain had stopped and the night was still. She craned her neck, squinting into the darkness. When Ernestine's flashlight swung into view, she stole back inside. After a few minutes the door closed beneath her, and the security bolts slammed shut.

Aurelie dragged the blanket over her and buried her head into her arms.

Until she heard a soft bump on the floor of her room.

She lifted her head to see a paper airplane. She crept over and picked it up. It had something written on the inside. She unfolded it and read, "Look out the window."

Aurelie leaned out to see Rindolf, Rolo, and Frank waving from below. Rolo put his finger against his lips. He adjusted a coil of rope slung over his shoulder. His long black coat swirled behind him as he scaled the trellis.

Frank disappeared, and seconds later he was standing beside her. "Never fear, the rescue party is here. I hope I'm dressed okay." He held out his arms and did a brief turn to show off his fireman's outfit.

"You look good in uniform." Aurelie's eyes welled.

"That's what I think." Frank smiled.

Rolo clambered onto the window ledge. "Don't listen to him; next he'll tell you he's the . . ." His foot became tangled in his rope. He tumbled onto the cushions and slid onto the floor. "Hero."

Aurelie dropped to her knees and hugged her uncle. "They said I have to stay here," she whispered. "That the pier's not a good place for a young girl to live. I kept telling them it's not true, but they wouldn't listen."

"They who?" Rolo asked.

"Ernestine Bloomfield and her Society."

"She's always been a meddler." Rolo smiled and tapped his forehead. "We've found a way to *make* them listen."

Frank interrupted with an "Ahem."

"Oh, well, that is, Frank found it really."

Frank grinned. "We've just had a very interesting visit to the courthouse to have a look at those documents that allowed you to be brought here, and I discovered a small hole in the law that means you can come home right now."

"You have?"

"Yes." Rolo gathered up the rope and got to his feet. "Who would have thought old Frank here would finally come in useful?"

"Thank you, Frank," Aurelie said. "I'd hug you if you weren't a ghost."

"Seeing your smile again is enough of a hug for me."
Frank pulled an envelope from Rolo's pocket and placed
it on the bed. "The hole is a very small but very important one they neglected to address in court and are now
about to fall into." He flicked his head toward the window. "How are you at climbing?"

Aurelie smiled. "But the dogs?"

"Don't worry about them—animals are dead scared
of ghosts." Frank stood with his legs apart and put his
hands on his hips. "You're safe as long as you're with me."

"Our hero . . ." Rolo tied the rope around the leg of
the heavy bed and unrolled it out the window. "Let's get
out of here before his head becomes too big for his puny
body to hold up."

It was 2 a.m. when they arrived at the pier.

Aurelie kissed her uncles goodnight and climbed
the stairs to Lilliana's bedroom.

She gently kissed her grandmother's cheek. "Lilliana.
It's me. Aurelie."

"Eh? What is it . . . who?"

"I'm back."

Lilliana focused slowly on her granddaughter. "Oh . . .
Oh my dear." She began to cry. "Is it really you? How did
you get here? Have you run away?"

"Sort of. Rolo, Rindolf, and Frank came to rescue

me, and they say the courts will never be able to take me away again."

"Are you sure? Because I'll give up the pier—anything I have—to keep you close."

Lilliana sniffed and lifted the duvet. Aurelie kicked off her shoes and climbed inside, sinking into its familiar warmth. "We're not leaving. I have a plan to make sure of that. Rindo says you haven't been well."

"It is nothing. I just . . . got a bit of a scare when . . ."

"I'm here now and this is where I'm going to stay for a very long time."

Aurelie wriggled further into her grandmother's arms. Lulled by the gentle stroking of her cheek and the duck-down quilts, she was drawn into a deep sleep.

An Unpleasant Morning

What do you mean the child has *gone*?" Mayor Bog gripped his newspaper tightly after Mrs. Farnhumple delivered the news.

"Miss Bloomfield went up to her room this morning and she wasn't there. And she found this." The principal held out a letter. It was written on fine paper below the name and insignia of a London law office.

Julius stood by the door of Mayor Bog's office like a nervous schoolboy. A twitch began in his eye, which he tried to stop with firm blinking. Had Mayor Bog looked up, it might have appeared that the boy was winking at him.

Mayor Bog dropped the newspaper and began to read the letter.

"Ernestine has no idea how it got there." Mrs. Farnhumple clutched her hands together. "She assures me the girl's room was locked and that her guard dogs are normally very good and . . ."

Mrs. Farnhumple continued to talk while Mayor Bog read the letter silently with clenched teeth and pursed lips:

. . . and, as you must understand, all processes of a legal nature must be carried out in full accordance with the law. It therefore stands that the child in question, Miss Aurelie Bonhoffen, was removed from her parents without the necessary documentation, notably Form 549B-2 entitled "With Respect to the Removal of a Child Due to an Unsatisfactory Situation and/or Habitation."

Hereon and forthwith, the child is to be returned to her parents and remain with them at the residence of Gribblesea Pier until such a time as the necessary paperwork can be filled out and a date fixed so that the full extent of the case can be laid before Her Majesty's court, in the presence of a judge and all elected representatives of both parties concerned.

Signed,

Frank W. Fotheringham

Frank W. Fotheringham

The Law Offices of Frank and Gribble, London

"And that is why I am deeply worried for the welfare of that child," Mrs. Farnhumple concluded with a sigh.

"I simply do not understand how one single letter can undo all the good work and intentions of respectable people who are only trying to—"

"Yes, Mrs. Farnhumple." Mayor Bog cut her off. "Leave it with me. I'll speak with my council colleagues without delay."

"Thank you, Mayor Bog, and again I am so deeply—"

Mayor Bog stood up from his chair and held out his hand to the principal. "Please don't say another word," he almost snarled. "I will see to it that this unfortunate state of affairs is rectified immediately. Julius?"

Julius's eye twitched again. "Yes, Mayor?"

"Please escort Mrs. Farnhumple outside."

"Certainly, Mayor."

Bog thumped into his chair, flinging the letter across his desk. Julius returned a few minutes later.

"This is a fine pickle, Julius. At least nothing more can happen to make my day any worse."

Julius took a deep breath before announcing, "I quit, Mayor."

"You what? Don't be ridiculous."

Julius squared his shoulders. "I thought working in the mayor's office would mean helping people. I never realized politics would be about rats and taxes and children being taken from their homes—so I quit."

"But, Julius, you can't be—"

"Goodbye, Uncle."

Mayor Bog's mouth dropped open as he watched Julius leave. He tugged at his collar and made his way to the window. He closed his eyes and took a long, deep breath. When he opened them, he saw Lucien Crook step out of his limousine. From the way Crook's cane snapped onto the footpath, the way he tugged down on his gold embroidered vest and strode through the front door, Bog could tell he knew about the letter.

Mayor Bog searched around for an avenue of escape. The closet? Beneath his desk? Out the window? His face paled.

"Bog? I need to talk to you." Crook barged into the room and sat down.

"I know about the girl. Clever plan, I admit, and it almost got the Bonhoffens to sell. But she is back this morning and they are again refusing to sign. She was even at the gates with those two scruffy uncles of hers, handing out flyers for some kind of performance. She's causing trouble, getting people excited. I want her and the pier taken care of."

Mayor Bog was finding it hard to talk.

"Well?"

Bog tried to compose himself and spoke through a rush of air. "I think the way to move forward now is to leave well enough alone. The Bonhoffens are obviously—"

"I want them gone." Crook's voice was low.

"But I'm not sure it's fair—"

171

"We have a deal."

"Yes. The deal. I'm not sure I want to be part of this deal any longer."

Crook stood and leaned forward, the stripes on his leg-hugging trousers immaculately straight, the cuffs of his shirt pristinely white beneath his expertly tailored jacket. He smiled. "You're too far in to be backing out now."

Mayor Bog gulped, his hand against his throat.

"If you don't get those wretched people off that pier by the end of this week, I will have to resort to *this*." Crook pulled a piece of paper from his inside jacket pocket. He unfolded it to reveal the front page of his newspaper, with the headline: "Mayor Steals Council Funds."

"But that's not true." Bog shivered. "I'd never—"

"Ah, but you see, Bog, all I have to do is print this in my newspaper and people will *think* it *is* true, and you are smart enough to know that even the hint of scandal will ruin your career."

Mayor Bog opened his mouth but nothing came out, apart from a small, embarrassing squeak.

Crook slowly rounded Bog's desk until they stood nose to nose. "Oh, and I always get what I want."

It was some time after Crook had gone that Bog's legs carried him from his office, down the stairs of the council chambers, past secretaries and fellow councillors who tried to catch his attention, into crisscrossing streets and muddled alleys, until he found himself in the square where his statue was being carved.

It was late in the afternoon and the sculptor had left. The canvas tied around the statue had been torn off and flung to the ground. The face was splattered with mud. Bog slid his hand into his pocket and took out a handkerchief. He dipped it into a puddle and tried to wipe the statue off, leaving muddy streaks instead. He gave up and slumped onto a wooden bench.

Bog stared at the fine figure of a statue who was slim, had youthful cheeks and the solid, broad shoulders of someone Bog felt he could trust.

"How did we get here, Finnigus?" He sighed. "And what do we do to get out?"

Uncle Rolo's Letters

Aurelie was walking toward the school gate when she saw Principal Farnhumple thundering toward her like a floral-print tank. She stopped toe-to-toe with Aurelie, looming over her with nostrils flaring.

"You have been very clever, haven't you, Miss Bonhoffen?"

"I'm sorry, Mrs. Farnhumple?"

"Wriggling out of an opportunity many children would have been thrilled and grateful to have accepted. Making a mockery of . . . of . . . what is right and good."

The principal swooped down until her nose hovered just above Aurelie's. "And I don't know how you procured the services of a fancy London lawyer, but it won't be enough to stop you from being thrown out of this school if you don't start behaving in an appropriate manner."

Aurelie met Mrs. Farnhumple's rage with her own

resolve. The edges of her lips lifted ever so slightly. "I'll be the example of impeccable behavior, Mrs. Farnhumple."

The principal's left eye narrowed, searching for even a hint of insolence in the answer. "Yes. Well, I'll be watching you, Aurelie Bonhoffen. Just one move, that's all it will take."

She clipped back across the playground, through parting waves of children, stopping only when she saw Rufus Bog.

"Rufus," she sang, "how nice to see you. Please give my best regards to your father."

Aurelie watched Rufus flinch. "Yes, Mrs. Farnhumple."

"And that I hope he is in the very best of health." Her smile was so wide it almost flew off her face.

"Yes, Mrs. Farnhumple."

Sniggard and Charles waited for her to leave before they sauntered over to Bog, glee plastered over their faces like chocolate cake.

"Please give my best regards to your father." Sniggard employed his most pompous accent. "Because we certainly wouldn't want to lose his favor now, would we?"

"Indeed not," Charles added. "Especially as I am so in *love* with Mayor Bog. Ooooh, I'm quite giddy at the idea."

Sniggard and Charles collapsed into their own whorl of laughter.

"Imagine that, Bog." Sniggard struggled to get his breath. "Mrs. Farnhumple as your mother."

Sniggard and Charles shoved each other back and forth as Rufus looked to Aurelie. She lifted her hand and offered a single wave. Rufus waved back . . . right when Sniggard looked up.

"Let's go and say hello to Miss Bonhoffen." Sniggard smiled.

"No, leave her . . ." Before Rufus could stop him, Sniggard grabbed Charles by the sleeve and dragged him toward Aurelie.

"Kids are saying you were taken away from home." Sniggard was smaller than Aurelie, but his smugness always made him seem bigger. He walked around her, circling her. "What do you expect when you think lighting sticks and throwing them in the air is fun?"

Aurelie ignored Sniggard. It was the one thing he couldn't stand.

He clenched his jaw and leaned into Aurelie's face. "Maybe next time Mommy and Daddy will teach you some more normal habits."

Rufus gripped his hands at his side and opened his mouth, just as Aurelie turned to him and said, "Are you done with these two yet?"

"The Golden Child has spoken." Sniggard rubbed

his hands as the clanging of the school bell began drawing students to class.

"Come on, fellas." He walked off but stopped when he noticed Rufus wasn't with them. "Bog? Are you coming?"

"I think I *am* done with them," Rufus said to Aurelie.

"Good." She smiled. "I always knew you were smart."

"Is it true you were taken away?"

"Yep, but I'm back home now."

"Nothing bad happened to you, did it?"

"No, I . . ."

Sniggard marched back. "Bog? What are you doing?"

Rufus looked directly into Sniggard's eyes. "Actually, my name's Rufus, and I'm staying here."

"With her?"

Rufus nodded. "Her name's Aurelie and, yeah, I am."

Sniggard laughed. "Can't you find anyone better to be with?"

"Actually . . ." Rufus thought for a bit. "No."

Sniggard, for the first time in his life, had nothing to say. His face was a look of confusion and then anger as he shouldered his way past Charles.

"That was good." Aurelie's smile seeped into Rufus so that he smiled too.

"I've been meaning to do it for a while." He laughed. "It felt better than I thought. I've also been meaning to . . . say thanks."

"For what?"

"The compass. I never said thank you."

"I knew you'd like it."

"No one's ever given me anything like it before. Anything that old, I mean."

"You don't have to keep it if you don't want it."

"No, it's good that it's old. I like it."

As the schoolyard cleared, Aurelie's smile disappeared when she noticed Valentina waving to her from outside the gate.

"Who's she?" Rufus asked.

"It was her house I was taken to."

"Do you want me to come with you?"

"No, I'll be fine. I'll see you inside."

Rufus joined the last of the straggling kids going into class.

"Good morning, Aurelie." Valentina looked uneasy. "I know you probably don't want to see me, but I needed to make sure you were okay."

"I am now."

"Good." Valentina squeezed her purse tightly. "I want you to know that it isn't right that people are separated from the ones they love, and I'm sorry it happened to you—and that I didn't do anything to stop it. My sister and the Society mean well, they always do. They have certain ideas on families and raising children." She paused. "How is your family?"

"They're fine. They're better now that I'm home," Aurelie said.

"Yes, of course they are. How are your uncles?"

"They're good. Rolo's as feisty and stubborn as usual."

"Still." Valentina smiled. "Can you say hello to him for me?"

Aurelie nodded.

Valentina reached into her purse and handed Aurelie a card. "If you ever need anything, please call."

"Aurelie!" Rolo was in the circus tent with Rindolf putting some final touches to a wooden cutout of a painted castle three times Aurelie's height.

"It looks almost real," Aurelie said. "Is the performance nearly ready?"

"We had a rehearsal this afternoon, and I think it's just about perfect."

"Dudley and the others are so excited to be part of the show again," Rindolf said.

Rolo shook his head. "They haven't stopped talking about it. How was school?"

Aurelie sat on one of the tiered benches. "Mrs. Farnhumple wasn't too happy about what happened. Thinks our family knows some fancy London lawyer."

"That'll be the first time Frank's been called fancy." Rindolf smirked.

Aurelie paused. "I saw Valentina."

Rolo's and Rindolf's paintbrushes slid to a stop. Rindolf let his brush hover in the air, a gray drip falling onto his shoe.

Rolo resumed painting.

"Valentina, you say?" Rindolf looked across at his brother. "Did you hear that, Rolo? She saw Valentina."

"Mm, I heard." He concentrated on dipping his brush in the paint tin.

Rindolf leaned forward so he was only inches from his brother's face. "You don't have any questions you'd like to ask Aurelie?"

"About what?" Rolo shook his head as if he was being annoyed by a fly.

"About Valentina."

"What would I want to ask?"

"You can be an old mule sometimes."

"I'm a mule?"

"Yes! The most stubborn, mulish, pigheaded, ill-tempered old—"

"She asked about you," Aurelie interrupted. Both men stopped still. No one said anything. Rolo rubbed at some paint on his palm. She moved closer to her uncle. "She doesn't live in a palace or a fancy London mansion—she lives at Highgate."

"Valentina helped steal you away from us?" Rolo asked.

"Valentina had nothing to do with it. It was her sister, Ernestine."

"That'd be right." Rindolf snorted. "Always was an interfering old cow."

"Valentina's still beautiful, Uncle Rolo, just like you told me."

Aurelie glanced at Rindolf, wondering if she should say more. He gave her a nod. "What are you going to do?"

Rolo paused before he stood up and dropped his brush in its tin. "Nothing."

"Nothing? But you came back to tell Valentina how you felt, and now's your chance."

"But what if she doesn't feel the same way? What if she never did? What if—"

"You never say anything and live the rest of your life wondering 'what if'?" Rindolf waved his brush.

"When did everyone start thinking they were experts on what I should do with my life?"

"When you forgot how to live it properly," Rindolf said. "Aurelie's right. You were given this chance to come back, and what have you done with it?"

"Put up with you."

"Put up with me?" Rindolf threw his hands in the air. "And what about what I've had to put up with from *you*? You think you've been easy to live with, moping around and writing letters every night to someone who never gets them?"

Rolo opened his mouth to speak, but stopped. He slipped his hands into his pockets, walked across the ring, and pushed aside the canvas flap.

"Did we say the wrong thing?" Aurelie asked.

"No." Rindolf smiled warmly. "It's time he heard all that and since I've lost my painting partner, do you feel like helping me?"

Aurelie picked up the spare brush. "Do you think he'll really do nothing?"

"I don't know. He can be hard to understand sometimes. I'll give him time before I check if he's okay."

"It was nice of you to come back for him."

Rindolf shrugged. "I couldn't leave him here on his own. Who else is going to tell him when he's being a stubborn old mule?"

Aurelie smiled. "What letters does he write?"

"They're for Valentina. He writes one every day. Sometimes just a thought, other times they're pages long."

"What does he do with them?"

"Puts them in his trunk at the foot of his bed. Must be hundreds of them in there by now."

Aurelie dropped her paintbrush in the tin.

"Where are you going?"

"There's something I need to do." She kissed him on the cheek. "Thank you, Uncle Rindo."

"What did I do?"

Outside the tent, Aurelie saw Rolo at the far end of the pier, his legs dangling over the side, his head hung forward. She snuck around the back of the bumper cars to Rolo and Rindolf's room above the lollipop shop. She crept quickly up the back steps to a narrow balcony and tried the door, but it was locked. She moved further along and wriggled her fingers beneath a window. After two firm tugs, she yanked it open. "Lucky you two are no good at fixing your own things."

She slid inside and went straight to the trunk at the end of Rolo's bed. She pulled on the padlock, but it wouldn't budge.

"Where would you keep the key?" She looked around the room at the books piled on top of an upright piano, shelves spilling with clothes, and two roughly made beds. Then she saw it. The one place in the room that wasn't in chaos. A small violin hung from the wall.

"She reminded me of music," Aurelie whispered. She took the violin from its hook and heard something slide around inside. She turned it over and shook an old key onto the floor. "You're such a romantic, Rolo."

She turned the key in the lock and lifted the wooden lid. There, in carefully arranged bundles tied with different colored ribbons, were the letters. She picked up a pile and looked through them. On the front of each one was Valentina's name in sweeping ink, along with a date. She slipped them under her sweater, grabbed some change from a jar on the table, and hurried out the way she came.

Valentina smiled as she walked down the long drive of Highgate Mansion. Beyond the large iron gates guarding the property, a taxi sat with its engine running, and standing beside it was Aurelie.

"It's nice to see you again." Valentina unlocked the gates and pulled them toward her.

Aurelie held her hands behind her back. "I thought of something I'd like to ask you."

A stray curl blew across her face. Valentina gently brushed it away. "Of course. What is it?"

Aurelie held out a flyer for Bonhoffens' Phantasmagoria. "We're going to make the pier great again. Will you help?"

"It'd be my pleasure."

"And I have something that belongs to you."

"Me?"

"Yes." Aurelie swept the pile of letters from behind her.

Valentina frowned. "They're not mine."

"They are. Look." Aurelie slid aside the ribbon, revealing Valentina's name. "There are lots more back at the pier if you decide you want them."

"I—" Valentina's words snagged.

"Have got lots of reading to do." Aurelie handed her the letters. "Oh, and wear old clothes on the weekend. It might get a bit messy." She climbed back into the taxi and smiled as Valentina pulled the first letter from the pile and began reading.

A Dark Deal
by the Docks

Mayor Bog and his wife slept in separate rooms. Mrs. Bog complained that he snored the snore of the devil and sleep deprivation would make her old and wrinkled before her time. So while Mrs. Bog got all the sleep she needed, Mayor Bog happily moved into a room by himself. It was from this room that he stole into the late hours one wintry night.

He'd dressed in long underwear, woolen trousers and jacket, a dark cape he'd only purchased that afternoon, and a thick scarf. The winds from the sea, bitter and unforgiving as they sank their teeth into Gribblesea, snapped at Mayor Bog's heels as he wound his way down dark, cobbled alleyways. He kept the hood of his cape well forward over his head and his scarf firmly secured across his face.

Few people in the town ever ventured to the docks at night and, for those who visited in daylight, it was purely for business. Ships arrived with cargo from each end of the earth. Cloth, shoes, and spices from the East; fragile glassware from the islands of Gozo in Malta or Murano in Venice; lotions and potions from America and, at times, precious artifacts that had to be personally escorted to secure warehouses before they were unwrapped in the finest antique shops.

It was a forgotten part of town. Mangy and ill-tempered cats scrounged through bins in search of food scraps. Abandoned dogs limped nearby, hoping for leftovers. There was talk of murders and drunken brawls. Those who had lost their way in life were drawn here, left to breathe their last forlorn breaths in the dock's littered streets.

Mayor Bog was looking for a particular all-night bar called the Lucky Sailor that he'd heard about in late-night meetings at the council. A bar frequented by disreputable types. Types who, he was told, came in handy for "certain business" when all other avenues failed.

He found it tucked into an alleyway no wider than his outstretched hands. A small red light swung in the wind above its heavy wooden door. There was no sign to invite you in. If you were coming to this bar, you knew where it was and strangers were not welcome. Mayor Bog stepped carefully forward, until a rat the size of a small dog scuttled over his shoes. He flung himself against a wall and clamped his hand across his mouth, fighting the urge to scream.

The door of the bar burst open and two sailors toppled out into the lane, laughing and tripping and holding each other up. Mayor Bog slipped sideways, into the shadows, as they stumbled past.

His heart threatened to jump from his chest.

He took a few deep breaths, pulled the hood of his cape further down his face, and pushed open the door.

It took a few moments for his eyes to adjust in the dim, smoke-filled room. Only the bartender, with his hunched back and balding head, could be seen in a pool of light from above the bar. The rest of the patrons were faceless shadows. Darkened booths lined the walls. Bog squinted at figures huddled in muffled conversations. Others were slumped over, fast asleep on their crossed arms.

He approached the bar and lowered his voice. "Cicero?"

With a flick of his head, the bartender motioned to a man in the farthest booth. Bog was about to move but thought he'd look less out of place with a drink.

"Soda."

There was a snigger from somewhere in the shadows. The barman took a long time to shuffle to a dusty shelf behind him before he placed the fizzy drink on the counter. Bog paid and approached the booth.

"Are you Cicero?"

The man sitting before him wore fingerless gloves and chewed on a foul-smelling cigar, puffing clumps of smoke into Mayor Bog's face. Bog coughed.

"That is the name you call me," he said in a raspy voice. "Real names don't interest me."

Mayor Bog slipped onto the bench opposite the man. He leaned low across the table. "But you know who I am," he whispered.

Cicero eyed Bog. "I don't want to know who you are."

"Good. Good." Bog took a hurried sip from his soda. The bubbles tickled his nose, worrying him that he might sneeze. "You know why I am here?"

Cicero sucked in a breath over his stained teeth. "Yes."

"I have tried a few times to"—he looked around him—"to finish with this business, but this time I need it to work."

The man smiled into the smoky gloom. One gold tooth glinted in the meager light from above them.

"How serious are you?"

"Very."

"Serious enough to accept that someone may get hurt?"

Mayor Bog's breathing grew sharp and strained, as

if coarse fingers were slowly tightening around his throat. "No. No one must get hurt."

The man picked up his glass and drained it in a flick of his head before slamming it onto the sticky wooden table. He nodded to the bartender. "For that I'll need to be more careful, more planned, and that will cost you more money."

"How much?"

A new, excited glint shone in his eye. "Double."

"*Double?*" Mayor Bog said it loudly and attracted the unwanted attention of the other hunched patrons around him. The bartender chuckled softly.

"When do you want it done?"

"Within twenty-four hours." Bog leaned forward. "But there has to be a limit. I need you to cause enough damage to make it so expensive to fix that they'll have to leave, but don't ruin the pier. It's to be redeveloped."

Cicero snorted into his drink. "Looks like someone's been telling the mayor fibs. Word is, it's to be torn down."

"No, no. Mr. Crook said—"

Cicero laughed. "It'll be done after midnight tonight."

Bog looked to the door. He reached into his pocket and jammed a clump of notes into Cicero's hand, knocking over the soda. The man barely flinched as he held Bog's gaze.

"I'm sorry, I . . ." Bog used his cape to wipe the drink up. He drew his hood firmly down over his head and stumbled out of the bar into the bitter, salty air. His eyes watered as he ran through the cold smog and mist, winding through darkened alleys toward the lights at the center of Gribblesea. He tripped in his haste and fell to his knees in a public square. His breath steamed around him in foggy bursts. When he looked up he saw the nearly finished sculpture of the proudly posed mayor standing over him.

He felt the energy drain from his body. He pulled his hood down even further and ran without stopping until he reached his home.

A Terrible Feeling

A sleepy walk down the hallway of the Bog residence at 3 a.m. to visit the bathroom led Rufus past his father's study. A small finger of light crept from the barely open door and fell across the hall. His bare feet stepped cautiously toward it. He blinked to help himself wake up and sneaked a careful look inside. His father was hunched over his desk, his hair disheveled, his eyes bloodshot. He clutched his phone to his mouth.

"Yes, yes, I did as you said," he insisted. "No, this time it won't fail. Trust me, I—" Mayor Bog recoiled from the phone as if he had been slapped. "He says it will be done after midnight tonight—"

He stopped again, this time wiping a sleeve across his brow.

"I know I've said that before, but you have to understand that what you are asking is very—" Bog winced.

"Yes. You'll see. Within twenty-four hours from now, the pier will no longer be a problem."

Rufus frowned and leaned in a little closer.

"Yes, yes," Bog stammered. "There's no need to worry, I'll see to it that—" He slowly pulled the phone away from his ear. "It happens."

He replaced the receiver and sat with his face buried in his hands. Rufus waited for his dad to move. When Bog did, he strode quickly to the door, opening it before Rufus could hide.

Up close, Rufus thought his father looked smaller and grayer.

Mayor Bog patted down his hair and tried to pull some order into his crumpled and damp clothes.

"It's cold," he said. "You should get back to bed."

Rufus walked past his dad with soundless steps before stopping at the bathroom door. "Night, sir."

Mayor Bog gave his son a weary smile. "Night, Rufus."

"Rufus!" Aurelie sidestepped through the packed lunchtime frenzy in the hallway outside their class. "Rufus!"

This time he slowed to a stop and Aurelie caught up.

"I've been calling you," she puffed.

"Sorry." He hoisted his bag onto his shoulder. "I didn't hear you."

Aurelie took a handful of flyers from her bag. "I was

thinking we could pass these out as we walk through the yard. We'd cover more ground that way and make sure . . ." Rufus looked away. "Are you okay? You don't look very good."

"I don't think I . . ." He sighed.

Sniggard ran into the back of Aurelie with his bag. "Sorry, did I hurt you, Fire Girl?"

Rufus's body tensed.

Aurelie smiled broadly over her shoulder. "No, I'm much tougher than that."

"I'm glad." Sniggard tried to answer sincerely, but sincerity was never a trait he managed to pull off all that well. "Happy to be back home? Things must be pretty bad at your place if they had to take you—"

"Leave her alone," Rufus warned.

A few faces looked up from the swirl of bags and lunches.

"What did you say, Bog?" Sniggard edged closer to Rufus, looming over him.

"I said, leave her alone."

Sniggard and Charles turned to each other. "Ooooh, looks like little Bog here has a crush on Fire Girl."

Charles slapped Rufus on the back so hard that his bag fell to the floor. "Aurelie and Rufus, Aurelie and Rufus," he sang.

Rufus flinched. "Get your hand off me, Charles."

"Or what, Bog?" Sniggard's face hardened. He shoved Rufus in the shoulder. "Or what?"

"What's the holdup here?" Rufus looked up to see the perfectly straight black bangs of Mrs. Sneed, who was standing above him. "Rufus, what's your bag doing on the ground?"

Rufus eyed Sniggard. "I dropped it, Mrs. Sneed."

"Well, pick it up." She reached into her pocket for a hanky to cover her nose. "And you, Sniggard and Charles, move along—you're blocking the hallway."

Sniggard glared at Rufus. "Watch yourself, Bog," he whispered, before squeezing his way through groups of tittering kids. Mrs. Sneed followed, doing her best not to touch any of them.

"One day they'll get bored," Aurelie said. "They may even find something genuinely entertaining to amuse themselves with."

Rufus picked up his bag. "I have to tell you something." His face was serious.

"What?"

"Not here."

He led Aurelie outside and around the back of their classroom.

Rufus paced, his eyes flicking around him. "Something is going to happen."

"What do you mean?"

"Something bad's going to happen. To the pier."

"How do you know that?" Aurelie asked.

"I heard it."

"Where?"

"I can't tell you."

"When did you hear it?"

"Last night."

"At your home?" Aurelie frowned.

Rufus didn't answer.

"What's going to happen?"

"I don't know." Rufus's face screwed up. "All I know is that it's going to happen after midnight tonight. I don't know anything else. I promise."

Aurelie stared at his downcast look. "Does it have something to do with your dad?"

Rufus lunged, pushing Aurelie in the shoulders and sending her sprawling backwards onto the ground. The flyers fluttered into the air around her. "No!" he shouted. "It's got nothing to do with my dad."

Rufus clamped his lips shut. Aurelie pulled herself up.

"I need to get back to the pier." She shot a look at the out-of-bounds perimeter fence. "Don't tell anyone I've gone."

"I won't," Rufus promised.

The clamor of the schoolyard at lunchtime faded behind her as Aurelie made for the fence.

"The pier?" Rolo shut the door to the room he shared with Rindolf. "Why would anyone want to harm the pier?"

"I don't know." Aurelie sat on her uncle's bed and caught her breath. "All Rufus said was that he'd heard something bad was going to happen."

"Heard from who?" Rindolf asked.

"He wouldn't say, but he looked scared and sort of . . . sad."

Rolo sat before Aurelie on a small piano stool.

"Does he know what is going to happen?" Rindolf asked.

"He said he didn't, just that it's going to happen after midnight tonight." She paused. "I think it's got something to do with his dad."

"The mayor?" Rolo asked. "Why would the mayor want to do anything to *us*?"

"I don't know, but I think Rufus was protecting someone. When I asked him if his dad was involved, he shoved me to the ground."

"He shoved you to the ground?" Rolo cried. "He can't do—"

"It didn't hurt," Aurelie said. "He was upset when I said it, which makes me think it's true."

"The report to have you taken away was signed by Mayor Bog," Rindolf remembered.

"And the mayor's assistant was here both times," Rolo said.

"And it's his office that's been behind all the tax increases," Rindolf added.

"But why would the mayor want us off the pier?" Aurelie asked.

"I don't know." Rolo stood up from the stool and smiled. "But I think it's time we asked him what's going on in person. Don't you, Rindo?"

Rindolf saw the gleam in his eye. "You know, brother, I think you're right."

"What are we going to do?" Aurelie clung onto her uncles' inflating spirit.

"We're going to pay a visit to the mayor to show him we can't be bullied by his taxes and his welfare society women and his assistants with their reports and articles." Rolo threw his chest out and tossed his hair back in a dramatic flourish.

"And let's show him a little of what his life may become if he doesn't cooperate!" Rindolf raised an eyebrow.

"When do we go?" Aurelie asked.

Rolo paused and his shoulders fell slightly. "It might get a little dangerous. It'll be better if Rindo and I go on our own."

"You're not going without me."

"I don't think—"

"I'm coming, so there's no point wasting time talking about it."

Rolo and Rindolf exchanged a look. "Okay, but you have to promise to stay close to us," Rindolf said.

"Promise." Aurelie's smile lit up her face. "What do we do?"

Rolo grabbed a pen and a notebook. "We need to work on the finer details and, of course, decide what to wear."

"We'll need Frank," Rindolf said.

"Frank?" Rolo sighed. "If he comes with us again, he'll *never* stop raving about what a hero he is."

"Did someone call my name?" Frank shimmered into view on top of the piano.

"It wasn't me." Rolo crossed his arms. "And get off my piano."

"We've got a little job to do, Frank," Rindolf said. "And we need you to help us."

"Lovely." Frank floated off the piano and onto the floor beside Rolo. He put his arm around Rolo's shoulder. "Anytime I can be of assistance, I'm yours."

Under Cover of Darkness

A bent silhouette of a man rowed under cover of darkness. The night was still and deathly cold. His breaths came out in foggy bursts as he pulled the oars through the icy sea.

The pier stretched before him in the distance, faintly lit up by the lights of the town. Serene, quiet, and without movement.

He lifted the oars into the boat and rubbed his hands vigorously together, blowing three bursts of air into them for warmth. At his feet was an empty glass bottle, a can of kerosene, and a pile of old rags. He poured kerosene into the bottle, and with a calloused finger stuffed the neck tightly with a torn rag. Wedging the bottle upright in a corner of the boat, he made sure the cap was firmly secured on the can of fuel.

He gripped the handles of the oars and plunged them back into the water. As they drew him slowly to the pier, a small box of matches rattled in his pocket.

A Poisoned Confession

A thick mist curled into the night and filled the air with an eerie sense of unease. Of restlessness.

Of ghosts.

"How do I look?" Rindolf stood in a narrow lane, not far from Mayor Bog's house. He wore a pair of long black pants and a black velvet morning coat. He'd greased back his curls and swung a gold-edged cane into the air.

"I didn't know you could scrub up so well." Rolo's hand rested on the handle of a large sword. "And what about me?"

Rindolf stood back and examined his brother's high hat with a white fluffy feather, long suit coat, and bright, embroidered vest. "I like the touch of color in the vest."

"And me?" Aurelie stood before her uncles in her silk dress from her ghost train performance, complete with a bloody gash to the head. But this time she wore a long, blond wig.

"Is there a finer-looking young girl? Oh dear"—Rolo pulled out a handkerchief and dabbed his eyes—"if I cry my face powder will run."

"All we need now is Frank." Rindolf searched the dimly lit lane.

"How can a ghost, with all of eternity on his side, always be late?" Rolo complained.

"I'm here." Frank's wizened face appeared through the mist. "Just because I'm dead doesn't mean I don't want to look good." He held open one side of his navy jacket fringed with gold epaulets.

"Is that an ax wound?" Rindolf asked.

Frank smiled and opened the jacket further to reveal a deep gash in his side. "If I lean far enough over, I can almost split myself in two. It might come in handy if the old guy refuses to cooperate."

"It's unlike you to want to outdo everyone else!" Rolo's lip curled.

"Can't hold back my natural qualities."

"Are you sure you're going to be okay with this?" Rindolf asked his niece.

"Are you kidding?" Aurelie's eyes widened. "I've never been so excited about a performance. Now let's go save our pier."

The group of four set off. They rounded a bend that

led them to Bog's house, which was surrounded by a perfectly manicured hedge.

A hedge the uncles and Frank walked straight through.

"Hey!" Aurelie whispered.

Rolo reappeared through the bush. "Sorry. Forgot you can't do that." He lifted Aurelie over the hedge while Rindolf grabbed her on the other side. Frank disappeared through a wall of the house and unlocked the front door, opening it with a deep bow.

They tiptoed up the spiral staircase. All except Frank, who floated a few steps ahead of them. He wafted through the walls on the second floor, before silently beckoning the others to a room at the end of the hall.

Mayor Bog was in his bed, a sleep mask across his eyes. He tossed and turned, filling the bedroom with a rumbling snore.

"Looks like he isn't sleeping so soundly," Rindolf observed from the foot of the bed. "Wonder why that is?"

"Let's find out, shall we?" Rolo smiled cheekily. "Places, everyone."

Aurelie lay down on the settee and arranged her dress so that it draped gently around her. She slipped her hand into her pocket and rubbed her fingers over the smooth surface of the star ruby. Rindolf and Rolo positioned themselves on either side of the bed, and Frank disappeared.

Rolo leaned over Bog, pursed his lips, and released a soft, mournful wailing. "Ooooh."

Mayor Bog kept snoring.

Rolo wailed a little louder. "Ooooooh."

The mayor snuffled and snorted and rolled over.

Rolo frowned. He leaned in closer and let out another sad wail.

Mayor Bog swished his hands in front of him. "I'm trying to sleep, Mrs. Bog."

"Hmmm." Rolo straightened up, took a jug of water from Bog's bedside table, and poured it over him.

Mayor Bog leaped forward, lifted his soaked sleep mask, and ogled the two oddly dressed strangers before him. "Who are you and how did you get in here?"

"Oh, we're simply two men who'd like to ask you a few questions," Rindolf intoned in his finest cultured voice.

"Get out. This instant. I am Mayor Bog, and I demand that—" He suddenly became aware of his bedside table hovering beside him. "And what have you done to . . ." He waved his hands above the table. "How can you do that? Where are the wires?"

The table slowly lowered to the floor.

"What is happening? Who are you? What do you want?"

"What do we want?" Rolo walked slowly around the room, tapping his fingers before him. "Mmm . . . what do we want?"

Aurelie sat up from the settee. "We'd like some answers, Mayor Bog."

"Aaah! How many of you are in here?"

"That doesn't matter. What does matter is what you know about the pier." She smoothed down her dress.

"How dare you come charging into a man's house with your tricks and illusions and—"

"Oh." Aurelie shook her head and wagged her finger. "These are not tricks. These are the workings"—she wore a gleeful smile—"of ghosts."

"Ooooh!" Rolo wailed into Bog's face for good measure.

"Ghosts?" Mayor Bog pushed his sodden hair from his eyes and laughed. "I have met people who will do many things to get what they want, but pretending they are ghosts is the most ridiculous—"

"Oh, we're not pretending," Aurelie said.

Mayor Bog's blankets swept from him and hovered in the air before dropping to the floor.

"I . . . I . . . it's . . ." Bog shivered.

"What are you planning to do to the pier?" Rindolf asked.

"I'm not planning to do anything to—"

A row of books cascaded from a shelf.

"There was something I forgot to tell you," Aurelie said. "My ghost friends here get very upset when they feel they're being lied to."

Mayor Bog became indignant. "I'm not lying, I'm simply saying—"

Two long curtains flung aside. The double windows flew open and a cold wind blustered into the room, followed by Frank's wavering appearance.

"How . . . where . . . ?" Mayor Bog gasped.

"Watch what happens next." Rindolf sat on the edge of Bog's bed. "It's quite something."

Frank hovered over the mayor. He gave him a stare laced with sadness before lifting his shirt. "Someone seems to have given me this nasty gash."

Frank wheezed and staggered to one side and then another, threatening to fall on Bog. He groaned and gave a convincing, if not overdone, performance of a man dying in extraordinary pain while floating in midair. He fell across Bog's bed without causing a ripple of movement. Rindolf and Rolo clapped.

"It was a little exaggerated at the end," Aurelie said, "but you get the message."

Bog's face had drained of all color. "I don't feel so well."

Aurelie approached the bed. "Mayor Bog, the pier's our home. Why do you want to see it ruined?"

"*I* don't want it ruined." He hung his head. "Truly. And I never meant to hurt anyone, it's just that . . . the pier is wanted by someone very powerful, and it's he who . . ."

"Yes?"

Bog sighed. "He wants the pier . . . destroyed."

"Destroyed?" Frank pulled the two halves of his body together and floated to his feet. "How?"

"I . . . I don't know."

"Please, Mr. Bog?" Aurelie pleaded.

"I didn't ask."

"Who's going to do it?" Rolo demanded.

"A man called Cicero."

"Cicero who?" Rindolf asked.

"He didn't say. I don't even know if Cicero is his real name." Bog added desperately, "I warned him not to hurt anyone."

"Why would you agree to destroy the pier?" Aurelie asked.

"I don't know anymore. First it was for money, then—"

"Money?" Rindolf tilted his head in confusion. "You would do this for *money*?"

"No, not just money. There was position, and promises and guarantees, and . . . and . . ."

"Who offered you these guarantees and promises?" Rolo snarled.

Bog paused and closed his eyes before quietly admitting, "Crook."

"Crook?" Rolo turned to Rindolf. "The businessman who wanted to buy the pier."

"He said he was going to restore it," Bog said. "Make it better. Grander."

"So he'll have the pier whether we like it or not." Rindolf said.

"I never meant . . . it was only because . . . I should have stopped this long before now," Bog muttered. "What are you going to do with me?"

Rolo's eyes narrowed. "What I'd like to do is send you to the deepest, darkest reaches of a bottomless, tormented eternity. But, as it happens, you're much more useful to us here."

Mayor Bog brightened. "I'll do anything. I promise. Anything you'd like."

"You bet you will, and for now that means coming with us," Rolo said.

The group hurried outside, down the drive, and into the narrow lane leading away from Bog's house. When they got to the cliff that overlooked the sea, Aurelie saw a small orange glow on the pier. "Fire," she whispered.

Cold air burned into their lungs as they ran. Aurelie tore off her wig and hoisted her dress up to her knees. She sprinted after her uncles, her eyes fixed on the wisps of fire that rose from the center of the pier. Bog followed, wheezing and stumbling.

Rolo and Rindolf charged into the streets ahead, running through lampposts and parked cars, darting across the main street that fronted the pier, until they melted through the metal gates and tore inside.

Aurelie arrived only minutes later. She took a key from around her neck and opened the lock. She flung the gates open. The cold wind from the sea shivered past as her feet raced across the wooden boardwalk. She stopped when she came to a small cluster of people trying to put out a fire that was quickly consuming Argus's office.

Frank called instructions to To, Fro, and Amarella to lower buckets on a rope into the ocean, draw them up, and run them to the fire.

Lilliana had taken burlap sacks from the Funslide, dunked them in a barrel of water, and was slapping them against the boards of the pier where burning embers had strayed. The fire tore into the sky, snarling and crackling high above them.

Argus unwound the long, heavy fire hose. He and Rolo wrestled it across the boards and directed a stream of water onto the flames. Rindolf helped with the buckets while Aurelie ran to help Lilliana.

"Don't get too close to the fire," Lilliana cried over the hiss of the flames.

The faint scream of a siren was only just heard through the din.

The burning wood creaked and groaned. Steam drifted up from the boards around the office. The seared air and smoke caught in Aurelie's throat as she plunged her sack into a barrel of water and slammed it down on the glowing embers.

Bog stumbled to a stop and tried to gather his breath.

"Mayor!" Aurelie threw him a sack. "Hit this against any embers you see."

He lunged forward, grabbed it, and drenched it with water.

The flames licked higher into the air, throwing off bulging pillows of smoke.

Suddenly, a loud crack, distinct from all the others, fractured the air. The boards beneath Aurelie began to sag. For a brief moment, all activity stopped.

"Aurelie!" Bog raced forward and wrenched her away from the towering blaze. He threw her to the floor, shielding her with his wet burlap sack as the boards around the office splintered and snapped.

"Everyone stand back!" Argus cried.

Buckets were dropped in a rush to move away.

Aurelie and Bog looked up to see the office lurch sideways like a tree being felled. There was a small moment when nothing else happened, until the boards beneath the building finally gave way and collapsed into the sea.

A plume of smoke erupted through the jagged hole with a violent hiss.

Amarella and Lilliana bundled Aurelie farther from the fire. Along the pier, fire engines blazed toward them.

Rolo stood beside his brother, his fists clenched. Both their faces were black with soot. It only took one look between them to know what would happen next.

"Coming?" Rolo asked.

"Try and stop me."

The two uncles turned as the firemen jumped from their trucks and began hosing the last of the flames.

"Hey!" Frank called after them. "Wait for me. I'm not missing the grand finale."

A Little Spooking

I've found him." Frank appeared in Rolo and Rindolf's rowboat. "He's over there."

The two brothers rowed faster, following the direction of Frank's finger.

Cicero's boat was gliding slowly through the water after he'd stopped to take a drink from a small flask. He turned when he heard the splashing of oars to see a rowboat sweep up beside him.

"It's a good evening for a row," Rolo said.

Cicero looked away, grabbed his oars, and continued to row.

"Quiet and peaceful." Rindolf rowed to keep up. "Except for that noise from the pier fire."

Cicero grunted and focused on slamming the oars into the water.

"Don't suppose you know anything about it?" Rolo asked. "The fire, I mean."

"Nothing at all," Cicero muttered through a twisted smile.

"That's not what we think."

Cicero flinched at the man in the floppy black hat now sitting beside him.

"Where'd you come from? Get out of my boat."

"That's not very friendly." Frank frowned and looked over his shoulder. "Do you think that's friendly?"

Cicero turned behind him where Hamish, Glenda, Master Dudley, and Roberto were perched on the back of the boat.

"No, no," they said in unison.

"Most unfriendly if you ask me." Master Dudley crossed his arms.

"Wha . . . What's going on? Who are you? How'd you get here?"

"We're just a few ghosts out on a bit of a row. We do that, you know, us ghosts." Rosie floated in the air beside Cicero's boat. "Oh, and we know you're telling fibs about the pier."

"The pier? I've got nothing to do with the pier."

Frank held up the can of kerosene that lay at Cicero's feet. "What's this then?"

"What do you want?" Cicero snarled.

"We were thinking something along the lines of haunting you for the rest of your days," Rosie said. "That's fair, isn't it? For what you did to the pier, I mean."

"Sounds fair to me," Rolo said.

"It's the least he can expect." Rindolf nodded.

"Yeah, like this." Hamish floated up from the boat and transformed into a large ghoul with pointed teeth and flames leaping from his head.

Cicero clutched the edge of the boat. "Get away from me!"

"Or this." Glenda and Roberto sat before him as their skin crackled and withered away from their bones. They lunged at him as gnarled skeletons.

"Aaah!"

"Or we could—"

But before Frank could continue, Cicero dived from the boat in a frantic attempt to swim back to shore.

"But we were just getting started," Frank cried after him. "We can do much better than that."

Cicero's arms thrashed through the water.

"Well done, everyone," Rolo said. "That should be enough to make sure he never does anything like this again."

"Ha!" Frank cried into the night. "This hero business is great. I've never felt so alive!"

It was a few hours later that the man who called himself Cicero sat at the bar of the Lucky Sailor. The bartender stared at his ashen face and watched as his trembling hands lifted another glass to his blue lips. "It was hor-rible, I tell you. They came for me."

The bartender had owned the Lucky Sailor for over fifty years and had been witness to brawls, betrayals, and murders, but never, before now, had he seen a man so rattled in his senses.

"They said they'd haunt me for the rest of my days. They rose into the sky, enormous they were, with teeth as big as swords." He looked behind him. "What was that? Was that them? Did you see them? It was them; I'm sure of it."

The bartender shook his head as Cicero scurried into a corner of the bar and hid in the shadows.

Early-Morning Calls

Rufus!" Aurelie jumped up from the tables outside the waffle stand where she sat with her family. "You're just in time for breakfast." She held up a plate filled with a giant waffle.

Bog stopped. Rufus saw his father's face pale and his lips quiver. He grabbed his hand and steered him toward the stand.

"Mayor Bog." Argus stood up and offered his hand. His shirt and face were smudged with soot and his rumpled manner was more rumpled than usual. "And you must be Rufus."

Rufus shook Argus's outstretched hand and smiled, until he saw the burnt and gnarled hole in the boardwalk. "Will the pier be okay?"

"Argus lost his office," Aurelie said, "but he's already making plans to build a new one."

"And we thought we needed some pampering this morning, so it's waffles all around. They're freshly made. I hope you're both hungry."

"Oh, I don't think we should..." Bog's stomach rumbled at the sweet smell that wafted into his nose.

Rolo laughed. "I'd say that means yes."

"Please sit down," Lilliana said.

Aurelie shifted aside on her seat. "It'll be a squeeze, but you can fit here near me."

As Bog and Rufus sat down, arms flew across a table crowded with pots of tea and hot chocolate, jars of jam, jugs of juice, maple syrup, and cream. Two generously filled plates were quickly arranged.

"Are you okay?" Rufus whispered to Aurelie.

"I'm fine." She smiled. "But I'm better now that you're here."

Rufus concentrated on cutting into his waffle to cover his reddening face.

Bog sneaked a look at the damaged pier. "I'm very sorry about the fire."

"Yes," Argus said, and sighed. "It was quite a night, but the area is completely sealed off, and of course the public won't be allowed anywhere near—"

"I have no doubt that you will take care of the public, Mr. Bonhoffen." He drew in a heavy breath. "By now you'll know everything. I'm sorry that I—"

"Your being here last night really helped," Argus said.

"It takes courage to fight a fire like that," Lilliana added. "Not everyone would have done what you did."

"Aurelie says you pushed her out of the way only seconds before the collapse," Amarella said. "There isn't enough we can say to thank you for that."

Lilliana's eyes glistened. "Buildings you can rebuild, but this one . . ." She stroked Aurelie's cheek. "We can't be without her."

"You saved my life, Mayor Bog," Aurelie said.

"But I was the one who—"

"No point denying it." Rolo waved a piece of waffle in front of Rufus. "Your dad's a downright hero."

Rufus sat up taller and smiled.

"Rolo's right." Rindolf took a sip of his chocolate. "You should have seen him. He leaped to Aurelie's rescue, wrenching her from certain danger without a thought for his own safety."

"You did, Dad?" Rufus looked to his father.

"Anyone would have done the same."

"Don't believe a word of it," Lilliana said. "He's a hero and that's that."

"All we have to do now is plan what we do from here," Rindolf said.

Bog sparked to life. "Hopefully my news will help you out there. Earlier this morning I called an emergency meeting of the council, and we have voted unanimously to give a substantial sum of money to the pier, not only to rebuild after the fire, but for a complete restoration of what is a valuable and cherished part of our town. Rufus tells me you have a special performance planned. To make sure that goes ahead—and on behalf of the Bog family—I would like to present you with this." He took a folded check from his jacket pocket.

Nobody moved.

"Do you accept?" Bog asked.

"Yes, we do." Aurelie took the check and handed it to Argus, whose eyes widened.

"This will more than get us on the way. Thank you."

Bog's shoulders relaxed and he allowed himself a small smile. "We have also decided that part of the council's budget each year is to be spent on the pier's upkeep so that it will be in this town's future for many years to come. My assistant, Julius, once told me this would be a good idea, and I happen to think he was right." He stood up. "Now I must go."

"Won't you stay and help us celebrate?" Amarella asked.

"Thank you, but I have an important matter that must be dealt with immediately."

"Dad, can I stay?" asked Rufus.

"Please?" Aurelie pleaded.

Bog smiled and ruffled Rufus's hair. "I think that's a fine idea."

Aurelie jumped from her seat. "Thank you, Mayor Bog. We're going to make the pier better than it used to be, you watch." She flung her arms around him.

Bog held his hands in the air, unsure of what to do with them, before drawing them down and patting Aurelie's thick curls. "I have no doubt you will."

Bog turned away and strode into the sunshine with a smile and a step he hadn't used for quite some time.

"Well, that's put quite a bright spin on events." Rolo dug into another mouthful of waffle. "I don't think there's anything that could make the day better."

"I know one thing." Aurelie looked into the distance. Everyone followed her gaze to a figure in a long coat walking toward them.

"Valentina." Rolo let out a small gasp and dropped his fork. "I think I'm going to be sick."

"That's not going to make a great impression," Aurelie said.

"No," Rufus agreed. "Girls generally hate vomit."

Rindolf nudged his brother in the shoulder. "Well, what are you going to do, you great lump, just sit there?"

"I . . . I . . . but . . ."

"Actually, he doesn't have to do anything," Lilliana said. "She'll be here in a few seconds."

"Did you do this?" Rolo hissed at Rindolf before he noticed Aurelie's smile. "*You* did?"

"Someone had to," Argus said.

"It is about time, Rolo." Amarella kissed his ashen cheek.

"I'd say about fifteen years overdue," Lilliana added.

"Valentina." Argus stood up and opened his arms. "If you aren't a pretty picture after a pretty ordinary night."

"I heard about the fire. I'm sorry."

"We'll have everything fixed up in no time." Amarella gave her a hug. "Won't we, Rolo?"

Rindolf elbowed his stunned brother. "Welcome back, Valentina. Who would have thought you'd be even lovelier than when we saw you last?"

"Thank you, Rindo."

They all stared at Rolo, who remained speechless.

"Isn't it nice to see Valentina again?" Lilliana asked.

Rolo managed a nod.

Valentina drew the pile of letters from her bag. "I received your letters."

"My letters?" Rolo pushed his hair across his sooty forehead, only to have the wind mess it up again. "I'm sorry. They're old and foolish and I'm—"

"I thought they were beautiful."

"You did?" Rolo fell into another silence.

"He wrote them because he loves you," Aurelie blurted out. "And has always loved you and has wanted to tell you for years—and even tried a few times—but he just hasn't managed to do it."

"Partly because he's so stubborn." Rindolf raised an eyebrow.

"I'm not stubborn, I was—"

"You tried to tell me before?" Valentina asked.

"One night before I was even born," Aurelie said.

"You did?" Valentina asked.

Rolo opened his mouth to speak.

"He came to ask you a question, just like he said he would," Aurelie explained.

"We both did," Rindolf added. "But when we got there, we saw Reinfeld on his knee offering you a ring, so we left."

"I only knew you hadn't accepted when I read about his engagement to another woman a month later," Rolo said. "But by then you had gone to London. We asked Ernestine to tell you we'd stopped by, but when we didn't hear from you, we . . ."

"She never told me," Valentina said. "I would have come back, but there didn't seem any reason to stay in Gribblesea. Not without you."

Argus stood up. "Maybe Rolo would like some time alone with Valentina." Rolo's eyebrows arched upward and he looked even paler than before.

Aurelie kissed her uncle and slipped the star ruby into his hand. "For courage," she whispered.

Lilliana hugged Valentina. "Welcome back, my dear, and if Rolo forgets to say it, you're welcome to stay as long as you like."

"Are you going to stay?" Aurelie asked.

"If I can." Valentina looked at Rolo.

Rolo managed a small smile and nod.

"Excellent," Aurelie said. "Oh, and don't mind what the pier looks like now—it's going to be amazing."

The small group moved away from the waffle stand. When they reached the merry-go-round, they ducked behind it and watched.

"When's he going to kiss her?" Aurelie asked.

"Give him time." Argus peered over a horse's hoof. "They haven't seen each other in a long time."

"He's been wanting to kiss her for years," Aurelie explained to Rufus.

"Why doesn't he just do it?"

"He can be a little slow," Rindolf complained.

"I hope it's not much longer." Lilliana winced. "My knees aren't happy with this crouching."

In the next moment Rolo leaned over and kissed Valentina.

"He did it," Aurelie said.

"Well, what do you know?" Rindolf wiped his sleeve across his eyes. "He did do it." He sniffed. "With a lot of help from you, of course."

"Does that mean I deserve another waffle?" Aurelie asked.

"With as much maple syrup as you can handle."

It was a few hours later that Rufus sank back into his deck chair and rubbed his belly. "I don't think I could eat another waffle in my life."

"Give it time," Aurelie said. "I've said that before, but you always come back for more."

Seagulls swooped and garbled overhead.

"It was you who put the money in my desk, wasn't it?"

"What money?"

"In the envelope. For Mrs. Sneed's dress."

"I don't know what you're talking about," Rufus mumbled into his shirt.

"I knew you were a good person when I met you. Lilliana says I have a knack for spotting good people." Aurelie smiled. "I guess that's how I knew you'd help me save the pier."

"How?"

"Well, there's the good person bit I just told you about, but you've also been trying to hide for a while that you like me."

"I do?"

"Yep."

"You think you know a lot."

"It's a gift." Aurelie nudged him.

"Can I tell you something?"

"Is it embarrassing?"

"A little," Rufus said. "When I first saw you at school, I felt sorry for you."

"Sorry for me?"

"You were so different from everyone else that I thought it must be really hard to fit in being you."

"I don't think too much about fitting in."

"But Sniggard and Charles gave you a really hard time."

Aurelie shrugged. "Not everyone you meet will like you. Lilliana has said that to me a lot since I was a kid, and I guess it sank in."

"I'm sorry I called you a freak. I've never thought that."

"I know."

"And for pushing you over at school." Rufus sat upright and rolled up his sleeve. "You can punch me if you'd like. To make up for everything that's happened."

"I'm not going to punch you."

"You can. Honest." Rufus held out his bare arm. "It'll make us even."

"I don't want to hit you." Aurelie sat unmoved for a few seconds before turning and punching him.

Rufus lost his balance and almost tumbled out of

the chair. *"Hey!* I thought you said you didn't want to punch me."

"I changed my mind."

Rufus rubbed his arm. "You've got a great right hook."

"Juggling gives you great muscles." Aurelie smiled.

"Can you teach me?"

"Sure," Aurelie said. "It'll take time, and you have to agree to never show off."

"I promise."

"Friends?"

"Always." Rufus rubbed his arm. "Especially if it means never getting into another fight with you."

"You've got a deal."

A Not-So-Fond Farewell

A harsh knock sounded against the door of Lucien Crook's seaside mansion. After a few moments, Crook heard some quietly spoken words before the housemaid came into his breakfast room with visitors.

"Sir? Someone to see you."

"On a Saturday? Who could—" Crook looked up and his face turned the color of his newspaper. "Gentlemen? What can I do for you?"

Two police officers stood behind Mayor Bog and Julius.

"Mr. Lucien Crook, it seems you have been involved in some disreputable dealings that these gentlemen here would like to talk to you about," Mayor Bog said.

Crook stood up from the table and pulled his robe across his pajamas. "Now, now. I'm sure there's no need for this. Why don't we all sit down and talk about this like gentlemen."

Mayor Bog nodded toward the two police officers.

"Hey!" Crook struggled as the officers slapped handcuffs around his wrists and locked them behind his back.

"Mr. Lucien B. Crook, we are arresting you on charges of smuggling illegal goods, nonpayment of taxes, and the keeping of disreputable places of habitation for profit that violate the town's health regulations."

"You'll never prove any of it." Crook struggled.

Julius smiled. "Actually, Mr. Crook, I've been working very hard to find proof—and I was very surprised to find so much of it."

"There will be time to explain the rest of the charges to Mr. Crook at the station," Mayor Bog added.

Crook twisted and thrashed about as he was led past his staff and into the back of a police van. "You won't get away with this, Bog. Do you hear me?"

His voice faded as the van left the driveway and drove him to his new temporary home at Gribblesea Police Station.

"There are times when you do get to help people, Julius." Mayor Bog breathed in the crisp morning air. "Breakfast?"

"Yes, Mayor."

"And, Julius?"

"Yes, Mayor?"

"Welcome back."

"Thank you, sir."

Bonhoffens' Phantasmagoria

One month later . . .

Frank, I know how to do it. I was the one who created it, remember?" Rolo rubbed his white-gloved hands together. He paced up and down in his undertaker's suit in front of the Box of Incredulity.

Valentina kissed Rolo on the cheek. "It's going to be a great performance."

"Best we've ever done." Rindolf, also dressed as an undertaker, stretched into a lunge. "Now start warming up and stop panicking."

"And with me here"—Frank mimicked Rindolf's stretch—"it'll be nothing less than a roaring success."

"With you and your ego, it's like having two Franks in the room, when one is always plenty." Rolo rolled his eyes.

"You'd be lost without me." Frank kissed him on the cheek.

"Get off." Rolo wiped his cheek with his sleeve. Rosie, Hamish, Roberto, and Glenda giggled.

An excited hubbub rose from the audience beyond the curtains. Rufus and Aurelie sneaked a look.

"It's packed." Rufus's face was powder-white with large black rings under his eyes, and his lips were touched with a tinge of blue.

"It's like the whole town is here." Aurelie's face was painted just as pale. She wore a short black lace veil, long black gloves, and a dress that flowed from her chin to her toes. She searched through the crowd. "There's Miss Miel and most of the kids from our class." She gasped. "There's Sniggard and Charles!" They were sitting with their parents, excitedly poring over the program.

"What are they doing here?" Rufus frowned.

"I guess they finally found something better to amuse themselves." Aurelie smiled. "There's your mom and dad."

"I can't remember the last time they went out together." Rufus watched the two of them chatting and pointing at the stage and circus decorations around them. "Dad bought a boat."

"To replace the *Mary Rose*?"

"No, a real boat. He wants me to be his 'first mate,' and he asked if you wanted to come sailing too."

"I'd like that. You look good by the way."

"Thanks," Rufus said. "You too."

Rindolf peeked over their shoulders. "You remember your lines?"

"Every one," Rufus answered.

A clanging bell rang throughout the big top. The audience shuffled in their seats and whispered excitedly as the lights dimmed to black. A single flame came to life in the center of the ring, illuminating the face and arms of a muscled, tattooed man.

With a slight turn of his head, he gave Aurelie a quick wink. She winked back. Enzo threw the baton aloft, the flame spinning behind it like the tail of a comet. It descended in a figure eight. Enzo snatched it from the air and made contact with a large upright hoop and ducked out of sight.

The hoop formed a ring of fire behind Master Dudley Dragoon. "Ladies and gentlemen." He stood in an impressive uniform, arms outstretched. "You are about to be delighted, amazed, and bedazzled. *Welcome to Bonhoffens' Phantasmagoria.*"

Master Dudley raised his hand in the air and flicked it to the ground. A loud crack sounded, followed by a swirling curtain of white smoke.

When it cleared, Master Dudley had disappeared. The audience oohed and cheered.

Aurelie's smile flooded her powder-white face. "It's going to be a good night."